Meccano
Novel

Book: Meccano
Author: Aly Kotb
First edition:2021
Translated by: Marian Mccullough
Revised by: Khalid Boulbourj- Reem Alsrjany
Cover Photo by: Sama Abdelrahman
First Published in Arabic by Sharquiat Publishing, 2011

All rights reserved. No part of this book may be copied, used, reissued, whether in paper or electronic form, stored in a retrieval system, or transmitted in any form, without the written permission of the publisher, and may be used for educational purposes or to produce books for the visually impaired. Or missing it, provided that the house is informed. Short quotes used in presenting the book are also excluded.

Meccano
Novel
(Ihsan Abdel Quddous Award)

Aly Kotb

Translated by
Marian Mccullough

© 2021, Aly Kotb
Édition : BoD – Books on Demand, 12/14 rond-point des Champs-Élysées, 75008 Paris
Impression : BoD - Books on Demand, Norderstedt, Allemagne
ISBN: 9782322397808
Dépôt légal : Novembre 2021

"To those of you who are filling the universe with their creativity, it reaches us intentionally or unintentionally."

"The memory of humans is a pandemonium of unspecified possibilities, rather than their combination together"

Jorge Luis Borges

1

I dissolved into tears. This is the third time I felt weak in my life. The conflicted feelings in my being had been swept by the gray stream that went through my frailty and made me feel dizzy.

Someone knocked the door and asked to come in. I was surprised that I could not recognize the voice. His hands grew tired since they couldn't unbolt the metal knob. His attempts were in vain, as I bolted the door by the key so no one could see my tears. I went toward the door and my body went right and left like a clock that had finished its tour and its pendulum refused to stop. My steps were getting heavier; and the universe around started to spin. At my last step, I fainted and felt nothing.

-"what is the matter?"

-"psychological trauma, something distressed him and he couldn't handle it."

I understood the content of the brief dialogue. My sight followed a light that came from a small window by the atrium, I was still looking at things from the standpoint of a spider which was resting on its web and working hard to feel its prey. The web shook after a long period of waiting in part of the hungry hunter. The spider went to its prey.

The doctor looked at me with sorrowful face and said, "And what made him upset... what led a boy in his age to have a psychological trauma?!"

Disturbed by the doctor's bothersome curiosity, which had inspired memories that were meant to be suppressed, my mother replied, "His best friend passed away"

I closed my eyes, but a lonesome tear slid towards my nose and went to its final place resting between my lips... I tasted it; it was bitter since it reminded me of my catastrophic situation. The spider devoured its prey in zest, the pendulum stopped moving after small movements and the fish hanged in a small hook ended its protest and gave up in a tired compliance, announcing its satisfaction with the reality and fate.

-"That's a tranquilizer, let him take it every night. I advise you, in case he did not get better (God forbid), to take him to a psychotherapist", announced the doctor to my mother.

I heard the doctor while he was getting away little by little until there was nothing left but his monotonous feet then the noisy sound of the apartment door squeaking followed by a strong coalescence; announcing that the door went back to its normal position, I fixed my gaze at the light that ended its long trip in the wall opposite me, I looked at the body of the wall for a while, then I went back to my coma willingly.

In a desperate attempt to forget, I got up from the bed after a period that I could not identify, got around the apartment, and moved from the kitchen to the bathroom then to the bedrooms. I opened the door of the apartment. Whoever would watch, might think that I was escaping in my bed clothes, I opened the elevator door. I entered and closed the door. I did not feel what happened after that.

My mother sat at the edge of the bed and tears were pouring from her eyes, while my father was standing by the bed side. His face expressions were changing so quickly that I could not understand them.

After they made sure I was sleeping peacefully, they left. I pretended to be sleeping just to satisfy them; I got up to open the closed window. The wind was blowing heavily and the sky was pouring drops of rain.

2

We drove the car speedily on the road. I was listening to the sound of the drops of rain as they crushed against the floor; the weather was really bad... I closed my jacket zipper to protect myself from this cursed wind shaking me off. I began following the quick movements of Adel's car wipers, while thinking of who was behind making us travel to Alexandria now. Maybe it was Khaled or "Strong Desire", as I nicknamed him!! I came across this name while watching a foreign movie; one of the characters had the same moral features of Khaled. The other one who encouraged this bad idea was Adel. He prepared for Khaled all the suitable circumstances; the car, the apartment over there, Baker, the doorman. All those circumstances made Khaled cling to his idea. For me, I wasn't enthusiast about this trip but when I thought about it for a while; I decided to travel with them. We are together all the time, our projects are one, and sometimes we have these common crazy ideas. But today I felt strange as it was the pressuring force.

I cut into the silence that had overwhelmed

the atmosphere and said: "We must rest as soon as we arrive there."

"Are we going there to rest?!" said Adel.

I cursed him secretly, since his desire prevented him from thinking about anything else now.

"What do you think?" I asked Adel.

"I don't think about anything now. You decide and I agree"

I knew this very well; Adel was taking the side of Khaled.

Silence took over once again, cut by the sound of the rain pouring upon the car. Two hours ago, we stood by the doorstep of Kareem's house, he came to us, we told him where we were going, but he refused to come with us. "If it is about money I could lend you some" I said it sarcastically! As I knew his father's condition; the latter could buy me and my family as well.

He smiled and said: "Frankly, I don't want to. I decided to give up, I asked a religious person and he told me that there are other activities that can prevent me from doing such things"

-"But these things are forbidden as well", said Khaled.

-"You think that things are like fasting or regularly praying" I told him

-"Kareem, I know what you mean, but I

heard Sheikh on television saying that he who masturbates is cursed"

-"And which one of us didn't do it before?!"

-"No one, but not like the way you do. You do it constantly. You know, even after you get married, you will still love this habit"

-"Enough... Khaled, leave him, He is free", I said it to end that fruitless conversation, Each one of them had his distorted information and I was not better than them to interfere in the religious matters they were talking about.

After Kareem had invited us to come to his house for a little bit, we said bye. Khaled refused firmly the invitation, saying that he was in a hurry. Kareem said, "Send my regards to Bakr", before he disappeared from our sight.

We arrived at our destination; we came close to [1]El-Montzah as Adel's family apartment was there. Khaled smiled, I smiled too. I laughed at Khaled since he was getting himself ready now. The car stopped in front of this towering building, we got off.

The weather began to calm down and the rain stopped, I called Bakr as he knew my voice well, Khaled went toward the room and knocked on the door, Bakr came out and he seemed unhappy,

---

1- El-Montzah: A neighborhood in Alexandria

but when he saw us, he drew a big, bright smile that swept away the sorrow that was on his face. He knew well that we were one of his income sources, our presence meant that his pocket would no longer be empty, "welcome... welcome... why did not you say you were coming... I would have spread sand on the road", said Bakr.

-"anyways, Bakr... you know our demand very well"

-"Do you think you will find anything now. We are close to dawn"

-"I am your servant, sirs. But if you want it right now. You have to pay extra money, but if you can wait till tomorrow that will be better and will be cheaper for you."

"Damn you Bakr; you are acting as if you were worried about our money!"

-"No... It's necessary now. You always get what you ask for".

-"Ok, sir Khaled, half an hour and you will find what you want"

We went to the apartment, Adel kept searching for on his pocket but he couldn't find it.

-"Stupid... you should have made sure you have it, where are we going to stay?! At the neighbors' house", said Khaled.

-"ok let's give up the idea and go back," said

Adel despairingly.

-"you two are not able to think, there should be a copy with Bakr. Did he not rent the apartment to you at school time?"

A smile was drawn on Khaled's face, a smile of hope, he said; "hats off for your intelligent manner of thinking"

We stopped in front of the door till we heard Bakr's voice, he opened the elevator door, and he appeared with his tan face with the special scar on his forehead: "the girl is downward".

-"Let her up." murmured Khaled with his drool excitement, and then added, "First give me the keys of the apartment which are at your disposal."

-"Ok, Mr. Ahmed... right away... But before all of this, the girl wants a lot of money"

-"Why? Is she a high school student?" said Adel ironically.

-"Shut up... We agree on anything",

-"Who agreed? Talk about yourself, Khaled, we should know How much does she want, first?"

-"Not important, it's too late. It's her right to get whatever she wants, and let us see Adel's opinion."

-"get your voice down, guys, and you ,Bakr, let

the cursed girl up before someone sees her and this affair becomes a scandal, we are going to talk inside the apartment."

White beautiful face, excellent breasts, a butt that indicated that the universe was still good; she seductively put her index in her mouth in a professional manner.

-"Yes, she is worth it", said "Strong desire" (Khaled)

Khaled reached his climax, I believed if Bakr had brought him a dog from the street he would say about it excellent and would start negotiating with Bakr; considering him the dog's agent. "The excellent" started discovering the house on her own; she reached the bedroom with her sixth sense, turned the lights on, entered and closed the door. As usual we started quarrelling about who was going to go in first. It costed me extra money. We eventually came to a suitable solution for all parties. I would go first then Khaled and after that Adel. This solution made me pay extra in addition to what Bakr was going to take from me. I knew that very well.

He surely charged the girl with a lot of money; and he undoubtedly have accumulated a fortune by now. Khaled woke me up and said nervously: "Get in; we are not going to wait for a long time".

I did not argue with him. I went to the room, entered, I was sure of that; she had already taken off her clothes. She was still seductively putting her finger on her mouth.

I went towards her, turned off the light. At that moment, the prayer started from the mosque that was close to Adel's house, I turned the light on again and pointed at her to wait. After few minutes, I switched off the light. She didn't talk much and that was usually the way professional whores did. For them it is a career, they did not enjoy it but they were only interested in the income they received from it. Girls, who have sex for the first time, shiver and feel frightened initially, but gradually they break the psychological barriers and become professionals in the business.

I have memorized these steps by heart, I got a little bit of sexual pleasure out of them. Time passed by quickly. I finished what I was doing... I heard her voice for the first time; she said: "are you done. You are so quick".

"Yes, that's my habit... what do you want..." she slept on her stomach implying that she wanted anal sex. I understood the gesture and refused it totally.

-"we will add this to the sinful act we have already did!" I continued, "No, you can ask someone else. That's enough filth for me for today"

I got up and turned on the light, wore my clothes, she pointed at me while I was opening the door to let the next directly in. I heard Khaled's foot coming close, he came in with an enormous smile on his face. I went to the bathroom, took of my clothes, and went under the water to purify my body from this act. But would it cleanse my soul?! I closed my eyes; perhaps this water would be poured inside my soul. Perhaps I might get rid of that sinful boy, who just committed that sin, and who once thought he would never do it! Why did he do that? Why was he doing this sin? Why did he follow their lead in doing such sinful deeds and was even the first to do? There is still innocence inside us. I went out of the bathroom, I heard the door bell ringing; Bakr brought some food, he came in without saying a word, he put the bags and then went outside quickly. I heard groans coming from the room, Khaled felt happy since he was the kind of person, who loved to hear these alluring sounds. The whore charged him with money for uttering such sounds. The paid-for moans compensated for the flaw in his manliness and satisfied his sadism. The groans continued, as I went far from the room; went to sit down with Adel who was searching the food bags. I got a big bag of chips. I opened it, put it aside and looked at the rest of the food, which Bakr brought.

-"Look! The son of the bitch did not bring ketchup" I told Adel, angrily.

- "Eat... you are not going to die without ketchup."

I started to devour the food with fake expression of anger on my face. I closed my eyes and slept for a little bit. I woke up by a strong shake from Khaled's hand and his voice, "Money, the girl is leaving" .I cursed him; saying outrageously" Do not you know how to take what you want from my wallet without waking me up!" I closed my eyes again. I woke up to the sound of the doorbell, Bakr asked us if we needed anything. Khaled thanked him. I looked at my watch to find it was past eight

-The man in charge of the filthy missions became so greedy, Said Khaled.

-"It is not something new"

The three days went by. We were once again in the car; thinking of what we had done. Three days with three different girls, we went to Alexandria for lust, that's what Khaled wanted... Although there was a suitable place in Cairo which was my house, I refused to let whore into my house. So, we went to Alexandria where Adel's empty apartment existed. Adel's parents only stayed in the apartment in summertime; Bakr was the only person there whom we knew. He was the only one capable of doing such things.

Although we were unashamed, we were a bit shy; we couldn't talk to girls about such things. Notwithstanding my thoughts, I smiled. Yes, I smiled for what we went through and what had happened to us. Did we really reach that level?! Sex made us travel all this distance and pay all this money. Our sexual impulses were controlling us.

I closed my eyes one more time and I said, "Wake me up when we arrive, no one should wake me up before that"

I sank into darkness, seeing strange dreams... graves and hungry dogs... Dead became alive and ghosts were running wild in contaminated places.

Strong shakes awakened me. "Only ten minutes left before arriving at home", said Khaled. After a period of time which I could not identify; the car stopped and I got off.

"Bye" I said it and went up to the apartment, the memories of the three days were trying to take over my latent senses and my tired head, I opened the window to let the light into the apartment, hoping it might sweep away those three dark steel whirlpools which struggled to besiege my vision.

3

I was sound asleep before I was awakened by the chilling coldness that pinched my body; I stood up and closed the window. I went back to my bed, the rain was still heavy, winter was heavy that year and sad as well. Everything was calling for depression. I was thinking about going to meet Khaled, I did not know if I could complete the journey or not... that was not important, I was going to him, I did not want to talk to him on the phone. I wanted to see him, I saw his condition, and how did Adel's death affected him?! I went towards the car keys that were placed upon the small table. I took my phone in case someone decided to check on me.

I started my father's car engine and drove it without fear that my destiny could be like Adel's. It was almost five and half in the morning, I reckoned that Khaled could not sleep. Warmness was the best solution in this time. I was sure he was at home and he could not sleep, his situation was almost like mine, maybe my situation was worse; Adel was close to me since I knew many things, which Khaled was unaware of. And there were things that Khaled did not know, like Dalia's story. I stopped the car, went inside the big building. The old doorman saw me. He would usually begin his day after performing his El Fajr prayer and ended it subsequent to praying El Isha prayer.

-"I am going to Khaled", I said.

-"But he is not upstairs. He has disappeared for almost three days!"

- "If you see him, tell him to call Ahmed."

-"Ok"

He had disappeared for almost three days, from the accident day, I did not know much of the details but Khaled knew because he was the last one to meet Adel.

I looked around me, rain calmed down completely and the light was taking over again. A thought crossed my mind; to go to Kareem as he would commonly woke up by dawn with his father, he worked in the big species shop with him. The shop was visited by great personalities. This is what Kareem told us before. I entered the shop and found him sitting, looking at me; unable to believe his eyes as if I came from another planet.

-"The last person I was expected to see is you!"

-"I need to talk to anyone, I went to Khaled,

but he was not home, so I came to you."

-"The story of Khaled's disappearance is complicated. His father came to me; he asked all his friends about him, but sadly no one knows his whereabouts".

-"Where do you think Khaled went?"

-"I cannot tell. You and Adel, God have mercy on his soul, were close to him. So you should be the one who knows".

-"Me? Know from where? Do not you know my condition?!"

-"I know your condition and Khaled's. Last time I had seen him was at the funeral."

-"Did you go?"

-"Sure, it was so difficult. He became silent and tried not to remember the event."

-"How was Khaled?!"

-"Bad... That day I went back home and suffered from nervous breakdown"

-"What then?"

-"I mostly did nothing, I do not know anything about you or him till I saw you now".

I left Kareem after a short period of silence, I said bye with unobvious voice. I looked at my watch, scrutinized its glass; there was a crack at the glasses that looked like watercourse on its movement, it divided that screen into two halves.

It was seven thirty; I moved towards the car.

Khaled opened the door, I got in where I usually sit at the back seat. Adel looked at us and said; "I did not sleep for two days so either I will drive you into a pave or hit someone."

-"You say that every time. Yet, we always arrive safely to our homes"

-"I just want to warn you."

Be careful.…. the voice of a passerby, I pressed the brakes quickly. I felt nothing but flying papers, bleeding child and passersby surrounding me, and lost dreams.

4

-"It is going to be fine, God willing."

-"He is going to miss his exam because of you"

-"I surely meant no harm. Besides, He was not paying attention to the road, while he was crossing it."

We finished this small conversation. We both sat in the big waiting room, while the mother was standing in front of the room, waiting for the doctor to come out.

I looked at my watch; I noticed that it was eight fifteen .So, I asked his father; "When is he supposed to sit for the exam?" He agitatedly answered, "At nine." I then added," So, there is still time left for him to sit for the exam. That's of course if he is okay."

The doctor came out of the room and comforted them, "Thank God; he is good. The injuries he sustained were all superficial and he may get out tomorrow." I quickly moved to do what was buzzing my head. The father panicked and asked me," where are you going?" I pointed at him to wait but he followed me as he was worried that I would run away, He got into the car with me. We drove to the school.

-"Thank God, The headmistress was very respectful" I said, "it was good that she allowed him to sit for the exam at the hospital"

At this moment, my father and my mother arrived. And panic appeared on their faces.

-"Aren't you going to stop being crazy, you are no longer normal. You are mad!!"

I could not speak at that time. I expressed only my dismay at what Kareem had done with that old doorman; it was utterly inappropriate. I saw the tears pouring from the doorman's eyes. I turned my face to the other side so that I would not see his weakness before my eyes, while Adel moved toward uncle Kamal. "Do not be upset, kind man... Kareem is like your son."

-"But my son would never harm me. Why did all this happen, is it just because I told him that he could not park here? Does that make me crazy as he said?"

-"No never, but maybe Kareem is a little bit annoyed... We should all put up with him."

-"Mr. Adel but you do not accept that."

-"Uncle Kamal, no one accepts this kind of behavior. You have been here ever since we started coming to the club; you treat everyone respectfully."

-"God bless you, Mr. Adel."

-"As for Kareem, I'm sure he will apologize to you when he calms down"

"I am so sorry, Father. I know I erred when I went out while I am still sick and made you worry about me. I apologize again". At this point my mother hugged me. "Ok, what about the boy you had hit how is he?" I assured her he was fine and told her all the details until tranquility appeared on her face, like someone who ate after fasting all day and waiting eagerly for El Maghreb Prayer.

At this moment, we heard the voice of loud screams. At this point, numerous voices were overlapping, they were not new voices. Someone died... God have mercy on his soul, the patient in room seven... Death is better than sickness.

May God have mercy on his soul.

-Be strong.

-I wish uncle Kamal had forgiven me.

Three sentences I, Adel and Kareem said in a row, while Khaled was eyeing the breasts of Salwa, the daughter of uncle Kamal, who was lying motionlessly on his bed, surrendering himself to God.

His eyes were facing the rickety ceiling of the room. I looked at Khaled to stop him. I mumbled some unclear words. We went out of the small apartment, which was located in one of the lanes next to Victoria Square. We offered to help Kamal's family in the funeral arrangements; but they refused the idea completely.

I wondered at the irony of fate; we went with Kareem to apologize to Kamal, we went at that time of his death, and what did this refer to? What was the divine message which our visions couldn't interpret? This was something that needed to be thought of carefully.

-"I think it is your words that made him die."

-"Adel, Are you going to impute his death on me. That is God's fate".

- "Guys, let's forget about this. This lecture should not be given to Kareem because he was intending to apologize today to the man for his hurtful words. Our speech should be addressed to the unrespectable person, (Khaled) who, oblivious of sorrow, depression, and outcries of Kamal's family, was staring at the breast of a girl, who still haven't turned sixteen yet".

Silence dominated the atmosphere after I had uttered my words, Khaled looked at the ground. Adel disapprovingly looked at me while Kareem deprecatingly laughed at Kareem. I got into the car with Adel while Khaled got into Kareem's car. We didn't converse with each other although I knew that both of us were angry at Khaled's brainless behavior. I arrived home. As usual when I went through hard time I closed the door with the key.

It was the first time I ever felt weak, I cried a lot that day. I felt that the incident was a warning from God that was directed to me or to someone else, who experienced the situation; we had to understand it very well so that we would not be punished.

I went to the child's room to make sure he was doing well before I left, everything was ok. I apologized to the parents of the child. I fixed everything; my father paid the hospital bills and it was time for me to apologize to Yasser.

-"How are you now?"

-"I'm fine, Thanks to God"

-"Did you perform well in the exam?"

-"Yes, I did, thanks to God."

-"I am sorry"

-"It is okay."

-"I promise I will come and visit you at home after the examination results are released. You are about to graduate from primary school, right?" I said it while I was laughing.

-"I almost died before I graduated from primary school"

-"God prevented it, Thank God. I am awfully sorry again."

I went back home, my father told me not to go out without his permission.

More than a week had gone by since that depressing funeral day, Khaled suggested that we should travel to Alexandria, since there were women, Bakr the sea. Neither I nor Adel approved of his suggestion.

-"Why do not you agree, we should talk".

-"Khaled, I am really sick of the degenerate things we are doing"

-"Ahmed, you are right. We are sick of Bakr; he is using us and the women he is bringing. I feel agitated towards them. Do you believe I saw one of them last week while I was with Dalia?"

-"Did she find out about what we did?!"

-"yes",

-"Where did you see her!!?" said Khalid nastily.

-"In Alexandria, I was with Dalia because for she wanted to attend seminar in Alexandria's library."

-"And you saw this girl in the library" I said.

-"Yes, she was preparing for her PHD", mumbled Khaled mockingly.

-"of course, not there, I probably saw her in

the street; she starred at me lengthily. I moved my face to the other side. You know, she came to talk to me and she said that she saw me before and she thought I was one of her clients"

-"And what did you do?" I asked.

-"of course, I denied everything. The whole situation was uncomfortable. I felt embarrassed"

-"The bitch embarrassed you. But what does she want by doing that?"

-"I do not know. It is just harmful"

-"Maybe just to make you look bad in front of the girl that was with you."

- "Maybe. But why would she want to make me to look bad? What did I do to her? Her behavior was very strange."

Khaled interfered in the conversation after a long period of silence. It is not strange at all, the saying goes like this; "blame her and she will accuse you of her sins."

-"First, the proverb has nothing to do with the conversation we are having; it is out of context. Second, who should I blame?" Adel said the second part of the sentence while he was smiling

-"I will tell you, but promise that you won't be upset",

-"Guys, let's think about why she said that to Adel, instead of listening to the nonsense of Khaled"

-"I know; maybe he did her wrong while they were together"

- "What could I have possibly did her that could be worse than what she had already done to herself?"

-Khaled said, "I will tell you, but promise me that you won't be upset"

-"sir, say and finish it" Mumbled Adel.

-"May she thought that Dalia is a whore, like her. So, she wanted to take her place, since she thought that she is worthy of your money because she slept with you before Dalia"

- Adel responded angrily to the remark of Khaled, saying; "Khaled, be respectful. How dare you talk like this way about Dalia?"

My phone was ringing at that moment, cutting the line of memories. It was strange. Dalia was calling me. Why me?! I answered after a moment of hesitation.

I felt pity for her voice, she wanted to meet me. I promised her. She insisted on knowing when. I promised her again that I would call her when I get better. She ended the call and I sensed discontent in the tone of her voice.

This was the first time I had methodologically thought about the accident, I had to help myself.

I had to overcome this situation so my family

would be relieved, before travelling again since they only had one week left for their vacation.

I have to think like Khaled. Where would I go? I have to review all his acquaintances so I could know where he is at.

I have to evaluate myself one more time. Sure, Khaled's father had searched for him in all possible places. I have to search in places he did not know of. I also have to meet Dalia. I have to know what she wanted and try helping her get out of her crisis, which resembled my own. Also, there are a lot of things that are not yet clear to me.

5

Mysterious faces emerge in our lives. We meet such people and think it is just for once and that's it. But they come into view once again and have an effect on us. They are divine messages that leave in our souls a barefaced mark in a manner that is either strange or exquisite.

People appear for once in our lifetimes and disappear promptly. We think that they will have a constant effect in our lives, but we move on and abandon them.

One week passed and the second followed my father and my mother checked on me. They commended my aunt to come from Ismailia every now and then to see me.

I laughed so much when I heard that. Has she even ever cared about me!! I knew she had lots of problems with my mother, quarrelling because of a silly inheritance, a small house next to the house where my aunt lived with her husband. My aunt asked my mother to waive her portion so she could demolish the house and expand her house. But my mother completely refused, my aunt was not convinced with the justifications of my mother. Anyway, what did memories mean?

Odd reason not to sell the house, her goal was higher than my mother's. At any rate, there was nothing to affect their cold relationship now; their relationship was at the edge. It was nothing more than some courtesy and exchange of words in occasions, like feasts and Labor Day. I liked my silly joke; it made me laugh a lot.

I did not know why my mother called her anyways? Was my mother worried about me that much? My situation is not that bad, at least not yet. There were still spaces between me and craziness but all the ways are leading to it, I had to resist fate, and I had to do something to escape this destiny.

The beautiful nurse met me with a reassuring smile, I asked for an appointment. She searched her list. She apologized for not finding any appointment for the following three days. I told her I was not in a hurry. I reserved a suitable appointment and left; not caring about her warnings that were all revolving around the idea that: "If I did not come in due time, I would lose all the money."

I came close to Kareem's house now. I remembered Mrs. Madiha, Kareem's neighbor, who lived in the top floor and with whom I had an intimate relationship three years ago. Ever since

I became friends with Kareem, I frequented his house. I met Mrs. Madiha once in the elevator; she did not see her after that for three months and I forgot about her.

I met her several times after that while I was getting in or out. This made me feel like those meetings were intentional. Madiha began raising my suspicions. I tried collecting some information about her. I knew she had been a widow for five years. She was working in an insurance company before her marriage. She left her job because her husband wanted that. Her deceased husband had been an owner of a renting car which his kids of another wife inherited after his death. They left her the apartment and some money. These are some of the information I gathered after establishing a relationship with her.

I frequented her apartment for a period of time, then she asked me to end our relationship. I agreed without hesitation. I wanted that and at the same time I did not. After we ended our relationship, Kareem told me that his father wanted to marry a third wife. He said it this way and told me that his father chose Madiha, as his wife. I asked him if his father asked her or not. It was not a surprise when he assured my expectations; he asked her a month ago at the same time when she asked me to end our relationship.

I left Kareem, knocked on her door violently, she opened with astonishment on her face, I remember this time very well. It was like raping with no feelings; I left her after I had rained her with a torrent of insults and curses. I felt nothing. I threatened that I would tell Kareem's father about our relationship. She held my hand trying to kiss it. She begged me not to tell him. I left without showing any interest on her begging. After I left, she tried calling repeatedly. I did not answer till she sent me a message on my phone, telling me she was going to commit suicide. I knew it might be just a threat but fear possessed me. I was afraid she would be depressed and do it. I called her. She did not answer the first time... I recognized it was a cold war; she wanted to play with my feelings the way I played with hers. I called her again... she answered, I told her it was over and directly ended the call. That was the last time I talked to Madiha... Madiha's story came to an end... or I thought it did.

I called Dalia. We set an appointment to meet. I thought we needed to talk. I did not meet Dalia only few times. She was a beautiful girl, a year younger than us. Adel used to talk about her. Adel knew her since he was a child. He used to mention this point a lot. "The most beautiful thing in the universe is to see the person whom you love growing up in front of your eyes. I cannot imagine life without her". He used to repeat these sentences recurrently. Since I knew Adel, Kareem and Khaled for virtually ten years, we were always together until Adel's accident separated us. I had spent almost half of my lifetime with them, a period during which I became free willed; capable of choosing and making distinctions between what I want and what I did not.

Five years ago, my parents left me. They asked me if I needed them. I preferred silence as the answer was known. They told me that they needed money and that their needs increased, I did not mind. Actually, I liked the idea of living and taking care of myself. I learned this idea from the western world. I was introduced to this idea when I was messaging Anya for a year and half, a girl who lived by herself too. (I could talk to her with some German language I learnt from high school. She refused to speak English since she appreciated her mother tongue more) When she visited Egypt, eight months ago, I invited her to my house, she strongly agreed and it was an unforgettable night, A European girl, very beautiful and me! What did I need more than this or what would any person want more than this? No, there are of course those who prefer Asian or Latin girls.

Adel mocked me a lot when he heard about the idea of chatting, "Oh. Our Fathers were doing this in the seventies and the eighties". This idea started when I discovered websites that helped in chatting. I uploaded my personal information and picture in the website. After a month, I got a message on my e-mail from Anya. We lived the story.

Dalia arrived on time, not like Adel who was always late. After some boring, conventional chit-chat, the important conversation started; I asked her about the details of Adel's accident. She answered that she knew there were some family disputes, but she did not know if these disputes were related to the accident or not." For this reason, my connection with Adel was cut before the accident. He did not call me and even when I called him, he did not answer."

I went back home after a meeting I learned nothing from. I cursed my hurriedness; problems were not going to be solved by hurriedness.

There were no surprises. Dalia was the

same. Adel talked to me extensively about her personality and mindset. He even introduced me to her once.

Confusion appeared on Adel's face, I did not know its source back-then. He told me about his dissatisfaction with Dalia's behaviors. She insisted on going to the book exhibition all time when he was with her and he refused that.

-"What is wrong Adel? Is this jealousy!!"

-"No, I am worried about her. Who would be crazy enough to go to a book exhibition every single day? People would usually go there once or twice, but when they do so every day, that implies a problem"

-"No, most people who go there are educated and respectful."

-"It is not a theory. Not all educated people are respected and not all respected people are educated"

-"Ok. Why are you worried about her?"

-"I do not know but there are a lot of people there who make me feel uncomfortable. In addition, some boys, who don't care about reading or anything, go there"

-"I do not know what to tell you, why didn't you persuade her to finish all what she want in one day or two?"

-"I tried but I could not. Besides, she told me that she has a lot of researches to do. Also, she is participating in a conference by the end of March. Thus, she is preparing for it."

-"From now? It's too early until the date of the conference!"

-"I told her the same thing. She gave me a lecture about the art of time management. And she acted like a professor of human development"

-"And the solution?"

- "I should talk to her again. May God make it easy for me this time?"

Adel did talk to her again and she promised him to finish her research quickly. I went with them for some days. Dalia was a student at her second year in college, majoring in English. She was smart and wanted always to be the best.

She was also a tennis player; I didn't know about her level, since I was unaware of the rules of the game. All I knew is that I had seen her in a match of the national championship of Tennis and I concluded that she won. I saw her happy after the match and Adel congratulated her, so it reinforced my conclusion. Frankly I could not ask her about the result so I would not feel embarrassed. Her distinguishing trait was ambition. That was what Adel told me. I recalled every single word that was said about her. I'm not aware of why these words are engraved in my mind, but perhaps, one day, I would.

6

Anya, the incredibly beautiful girl, finally arrived. She was as exquisite as I had imagined her to be, bearing the unsophisticated features of European girls. She knew nothing about Arabic. That was what I thought at the beginning. She did not want to speak English, she came to spend one week with me. That was what I thought at the beginning. She wanted me to show her all of Egypt in one week, she knew how to manage her time.

My real problem was how I could let her into my apartment without being seen, but Anya told me that her tourist agency had booked a room for her in one of the most luxurious hotels in the country. However, it was evident that I was upset because of that and she decided to come with me to my apartment. I was thinking of traveling with her. She kept encouraging me not to take that decision to the extent that she made me feel like I was talking to Dalia.

She was persuading me that my country is better. She started talking with me about her country and its achievements. She finished her speech and I started mine: "Once, we were ranked the fourth in the world championship for handball, Agogo played for Zamalek football team. We beat Italy in the FIFA federation's cup. This is not to mention the fact that we have won the African cup of nations for several times; we also constructed the great dam. We have the subway, beautiful sun and also an exceptional sense of humor. In addition, we are the only people in the entire world that love to spread their dirty clothes in space". She did not understand most of my speech, I thanked God for that. She started talking about herself and her family, the surprise was that her uncle was a journalist in a renowned German newspaper and she was a journalist like him or would like to be like him. Her speech ended at this point, she came with me to my apartment. I watched the way. Anya got in while I was standing on the steps watching and making sure no one had seen her. I got in happily.

Finally, we were by ourselves. I started singing; using random words and enjoyed that Anya could not understand me. Little Anya, Anya who has enticing movements, Any, I was saying these senseless words and she was shaking her head; wondering; unable to understand my strange speech. I was like a sorcerer telling his mysterious spells. She changed her clothes. We sit together, shared talk, then I began uttering my mysterious words again, "little Anya, Anya, the girl with the dangerous moves, Anya."

Yesterday was remarkably beautiful! Anya was sleeping, how beautiful she was! I watched her in silence. I bet she was not above her twenties. My cellphone rang, that was Adel. He called to check on me. I did not call him yesterday; I claimed that I was sick. He offered to come and visit me. "Do not bother," I said it to him. I promised to call him in couple days when I regained my strength. Anya woke up and we ate together.

She wanted to be with me the whole week. It looked like my performance was honorable yesterday. I said it secretly and I welcomed that. The best thing for me now was to stay with her. Why did I think of Adel and Khaled at this moment? I opted for Anya instead of Adel and Khalid. Did she deserve that? A question that I pondered upon deeply, till now what Anya had given me was too much but why did I stay with her? Maybe it was Xenophilia. I did not know then. Sometimes, I kept on thinking but without reaching any outcomes. When I sat down with Anya in any public place, I had a strange feeling, a feeling whose name I didn't know, But

I could describe it; marvelous! I sit down with a foreigner, who did not know anyone on this country but me, she trusted me so much. I sensed what officials call a feeling of leadership. What attracted me to Anya was the fact that she was from another country. But what I hated about her was that she did not have a soul; she was like a beautiful doll. Anya noticed a picture of me with Adel and Khaled. She asked me about them. I told her they were my friends. She showed me a picture of her with a young man; her friend from another Arabic country. I did not know why the picture annoyed me?! My feeling of leadership was gradually fading away. Anya asked to go out. I watched the entrance of the building another time and we went out peacefully.

When I was with Anya, she subjected to catcalls and it annoyed me. In the streets, some boys uttered some senseless comments. It looked like they learned nothing from the touristic advertisements that suggested that avoiding sexual harassment is for the advantage of the country. Anya introduced me to another friend; I could not remember her name as we did not spend with her more than one day and she suffered from sexual harassments as well. I remembered very well when I walked with her and Anya; I was happy! On my right, there was Anya and to my left her friend. This time a scornful voice came from behind us, "Flower, Jasmine and in the middle is the Flask". I looked back and saw three boys. It looked like what I, Khaled and Adel used to do was happening to me. I confess that they easily provoked me. All the people in the street laughed at me. Anya and her friend did not understand anything, I was so angry. I held a brick; and threw it at them. It landed in the head of one of them. I realized then how skilled I was in brick-throwing. I did not feel what had happened after that. All that I could recall was that I found myself in the police station. Anya's passport had protected me. She said passionately numerous sentences, what I understood was, "Those annoyed us and I magnanimously saved her." The guys stood hopeless; the head of one of them was still bleeding. We got out the police station, the police man was still apologizing and promising to punish those guys since they were immoral. I apologized to Anya for what had happened. She told me she was not angry, but was rather happy that she helped me out of this dilemma.

Anya asked me about some places. I inquired about the underlying reasons, so she told me about a demonstration, but I didn't know the reason why it had erupted. She wondered how I was not following the news. She told me the reason why she was visiting Egypt; an Egyptian got killed in Germany called Marwa El-Sherbini. Anya was sent to follow up the reactions of Egyptians. She was messaging her newspaper daily. At the beginning I expressed my annoyance, not because she did not tell me, but because I could've helped her so much had she told me. I suggested that we would go together to the demonstrations that took place in front of the German embassy or to the house of the family of the deceased. I was not surprised when she told me that she had done all this. All these traditional thoughts were useless since they emanated from a fiddling chap who did not like to think or who did not know how to think properly. What really perplexed me was the actions of westerners (exemplified by Anya), they did a lot of things in a short while, whereas we allocate only few hours to work. They work even while they are in their houses as well. I did not know why I am going through this useless contrast? I just compared people who work more than twenty hours a day with people who don't. I abandoned this comparison and started gathering all my thoughts. At the end, I reached an extraordinary idea that amazed both Anya and me and made me feel like I was the smartest person in the universe.

She refused to talk about ideas that inspired discussions about racism. She didn't want to open a dialogue revolving around them and she also refused to discuss traditional or overly-consumed ideas. Finally, she accepted one idea, the comparison of Germany with other countries in regard to these crimes. In Germany, these crimes didn't occur frequently, while in other states these crimes were recurrent. If I told her this idea stemmed from the proverb that says, "He who sees people's problems, will underestimate his own", she wouldn't have believed me.

After silent minutes, I suggested another idea; how jealousy from successful people would lead to such crimes, she liked this idea too. We started discussing the important points of her article, I did not argue a lot with her as I did not know the details of the incident because I followed neither television nor newspapers... I did not tell her that because I felt ashamed. All I told her was that I had a headache. It appeared on her face that she was touched by my state; she opened her bag, got a box out, and handed it to me. She told me that this medicine was excellent. I took one tablet then I gave her the box back, she refused and told me: "you may need it some other time."

I remembered that when we were at the protest in front of the embassy. People were condemning the accident and denouncing the racism that existed in Germany since World War Two.

Disturbance had appeared on Anya's face and she said some words that I could not understand, I told her about my unawareness of the meaning of the words, since I have never heard of them before in school.

I was utterly surprised to hear her say some Arabic words. She asked me in amazement about my bewilderment; I told her that I thought she did not know anything in Arabic. She laughed so much and she asked me why the newspaper would send her to Egypt without her knowing the basics of Arabic. I secretly cursed my stupidity. I asked her again why she didn't speak with that broken Arabic to me. She said that she thought that I wanted to speak to her in her own language. I told her for sure that was not what I wanted, since I was continuously struggling to understand her or to tell her what I wanted to say in her language, but that was her desire. Not only her but all Germans were proud of themselves. She got angry at me. She left me. That was the first time we fought, I waited for some time till she calmed down then I went to the hotel to meet her. I apologized to her and I did not know why I apologized? Perhaps I didn't want to let the chance slip through my fingers after I had seized it. I thought like that. Besides, it would be impossible to find a girl like Anya. After years of experience in life, I learned that I should never leave what I have till I find someone better or equally good. The important thing was that Anya accepted my apology so I invited her to my apartment again, she refused, saying that she was writing daily messages to her newspaper. I left her and went to a newspaper seller whom I knew. I asked him for the newspapers that had talked about Marwa's accident. I read all what had been written about the accident on the internet. The following day I went to Anya, and we talked a lot. At that time, I caught a glimpse of astonishment on her eyes because of what I had been saying. I waited for this precious chance to come for so long; I invited her to my apartment again and she agreed.

I implied to Anya that I wanted to go visit her country, but she did not show interest in the topic, and did not mention any of the words we use in such occasions, like welcome, your visit will honor us or you will brighten the country with your presence. She did not seem enthusiastic. So, I told her straightforwardly that I wanted to visit Germany. She asked me the reason. Frankly, I did not know an answer. Words betrayed my mouth. I did not tell her that Germany would be my starting point, nor did I say that Germany would be the land where I begin my struggle. Instead, I stated ironically that I wanted to see Zidan, the Egyptian soccer player of Borussia Dortmund, play a game, Anya laughed hysterically till few tears dropped from her eyes and not a single comment came out of her mouth.

The day of farewell had finally come. I did not talk to her again about traveling as I felt she was evading this topic and I did not want to look like a garrulous house wife, who continually talks about the same topic with her husband without getting tired. I implicitly understood the message of Anya without her saying it openly. The message was that you are not welcomed anywhere in the world but your country until the day you vanish from this universe. We have to deal with you. We have to have sexual affairs with you only to avoid boredom, and we sometimes smile at you out of courtesy; nothing more nothing less. We may need you. We study Arabic only to know your irrational way of thinking so that we would be cautious of your bizarre attitudes.

These may not be the thoughts that were circling in Anya's mind, but it was me who traveled with my distorted imagination far from reality; I was as ignorant as the author who wrote about capitalism, while he was drinking a cup of coffee on his office and smoking a cigarette, as what the translators of cheap stories usually say. I heard voices around me but could neither identify the words being said, nor was I able to recognize the words that were addressed to me or to the rest of the world. Anya was uttering indistinguishable words. The vague words were heading to my ears but lost their track and I failed to understand them.

I did not know why I felt offended by something which might has been unintended? I did not know why my condition worsened suddenly? I presented Anya an offer, but she didn't respond to it and I felt ashamed of asking her again. Her reaction took me by surprise.

It seemed like our number had witnessed an unprecedented increase, and thus, we were no longer us. It seemed like I had an ailment which I'm unaware of. I heard a voice that was not strange to my ears but I failed to identify its content, all what I knew was that Anya kissed me and left while I was sitting by myself at the table, talking to myself, while a passersby was bewilderingly gazing at me. They were suspicious pitiful looks at a young man, who felt very affronted, paid the check and left quickly.

He was collecting the shattered pieces of his crushed soul and wiping the tears that were scattered all over his face. I rode the car so I could see neither the road nor people. I closed my eyes and opened them, only to see heavy fogs. I stopped the car by the side of the road to avoid accidents and closed my eyes again.

In the night, I dreamed of a gigantic monster embodied in Anya. The monster chased after me until I was unable to run. It opened its enormous jaw and devoured me. I watched the process of digestion as it took place before my eyes and I was thrown from the other side. It was at that moment when I woke up, besieged by a sensation of revulsion and infuriation.

The dream reoccurred with its detailed features more times than I could count at night. It made me despise Anya and the days I had spent in her company. The beautiful memories I shared with Anya became horrifying nightmares, thanks to that dream.

I started remembering every word Anya had said and analyzed it with a malignant intention. I recalled words which I insisted she said it while she really did not. I was resolved to disfigure the image of Anya in my mind and substitute it with an illustration of a wicked witch who devoured children mercilessly.

Two or three days have gone by since Anya returned to her country. Ever since, I never left the house. I turned to my computer; I did not expect that Anya would send me that message so quickly, but she did.

"Maybe you weren't expecting me to send you a message as quickly as I did. To start with, I want to thank you for helping and supporting me... There were a lot of vague things in my life, which I could not understand previously. But now I am capable of clarifying them to you"

First, in regard to your desire to travel to my country, I will tell you frankly; it is very difficult to do that and you will be required to be compatible with many conditions , and it would be hard for you to do that, especially since you still haven't graduated yet.

No, I'm lying even if it is not my habit to do so, I can do something for you and I have to say this to you. It may be possible. I don't know and

I surely have no desire to know. All I know now is that changes have taken place and they now constitute our reality and the laws which we must abide by.

Like any other country in the world, Germany has its distinguishing trait (Everyone says the same about their countries; except for arrogant people who maintain that their countries are different). Once you hear the topic of racism, the first country that will cross your mind will be Germany and we both know the reasons why. Even if time goes by, this feature and others, which originate from it, will be ascribed to my country. Anyways, this is not our topic. What I want to say is that I may help you one day just like you assisted me during my stay in Egypt. I want you to try to be serious, try to stay focused or make your thinking positive, learn how to manage your life and time .Excuse me if I'm playing the role of the advisor, but I want you to try to bear me as I am writing all what is coming to my head. I don't want to look superficial to you or unclear, since honesty is the feature I revere the most.

Finally, I would like to ask you for one thing; I want to maintain our friendship, even if circumstances try to ruin it. I'm loyal to my friends so long as they are worthy of my friendship.

I wish you good luck and I am looking forward to hearing from you.

I wish I can promise you something, but it is better that I don't.

By the way, my article was published here and everyone admired it...Anya"

After reading her message, I had mixed feelings; happiness and irritation. I was happy because Anya's message seemed to have convinced me, and upset because she delayed this response and she pinpointed some weaknesses, which I knew by heart and longed to get rid of.

I thought a lot about a suitable response. I waited for hours until I found a response that seemed comfortable to me.

I wrote to Anya about my strong desire to continue this beautiful friendship. I wrote to her as well that I would try to upgrade myself. I thanked her for the advice and the dose of support she gave me. I told her that I would not forget the days we had spent together. I finished my message with stamps which I saved from high school days. I recalled, at that moment, the instructions of language teachers, when they told about some expressions that are used in the closing stages of messages.

I did not know why I felt like I was still a teen. My decision could be altered by a single word. I hoped that my self-confidence would be boosted in the upcoming days.

I got books related to human development from Adel, who brought them from Dalia. He was bewildered by my demand as he knew that reading was not my hobby and he said, "Your culture is visual. Besides, do you know how to read?" I laughed a lot. I took the books from him and read most of them. They all revolved around one idea; which is that in order for a person to be successful, he just needs to say so; I can be rich, I can be successful, and I can be happy. Our willingness to succeed differs, as teachers of cooking assert. This is the lesson I learned from these books and I have never realized until now.

7

"My name is Ahmed. I am twenty years old. I have a serious problem." These words came out of my mouth dispersedly. I tried to be strong. I think I was in a better state before coming to this ominous clinic. The doctor asked me to be strong. I gathered the scattered pieces of my shattered soul. My eyes became red as a normal reaction for what I had done. The doctor asked me to continue talking. He asked me to express whatever ideas that crossed my mind.

"We were four friends Ahmed, Adel, Khaled and Kareem. Adel died. That was a real thing. My problem does not lie in the fact that I sometimes see him after his death, because I know that the deceased never come back to life; I'm not a schizophrenic; I know my problem very well but I do not know its cure, and even if I know the remedy, I don't know how to make use of it. My problem lies in the fact that I think excessively about the past. I cannot forget about it, or rather, I'm a prisoner of my past. I want to go beyond the closed circle that fate has imprisoned me in"... I remained silent for few seconds; then the doctor smiled with an assuring grin and nodded with his head; instructing me to continue.

I told you; "Adel died. But what ills my heart the most is the disappearance of Khaled. He disappeared at a time when I needed him the most. He disappeared and left me flopping in the darkness. Frankly, I did not try to look for him. I do not have the strength to look for anyone. I need to look for me and help myself overcome this dilemma"

"I reckon that Kareem withdrew quietly. I think he did not feel anything. He kept slowly pulling away from us until he finally withdrew now. He was not saddened that much by the bereavement of Adel. As for Khaled, he is now independent. Kareem had recently grown accustomed to the absence of Khaled and Adel, while I, even when I was absent, would always meet up with them and we would do something crazy or carry out an odd ritual together, like singing in public. People looked at us suspiciously when we did that. I learned from Adel an important lesson; always do what you like without paying attention to the judgments of people; I learned that if you overlook the presence of people, they will overlook your existence as well. Do as you like as long as you are not violating the laws and act indifferently to the statements of people."

"That is a beautiful speech. You know I wish I had seen your friend Adel."

"I will tell you something a close friend of mine told me; life is like a scary movie. When you focus on the details of life, you won't consider it to be scary at all, but if you close your eyes, you will imagine and see things that are frightening. What I want to tell you is this, do not think about the past. Unlike what is commonly known, the past is not a narrow prison. Past is a wide dress, but it is meticulously tailored .You have to look at every detail in your memory and pave the way for future to escape this maze and think of what is new."

I looked at my watch and he asked me if the conversation was boring, but I assured him that our chat had positive impact on me. I really needed this session. For the first time in my life, I felt that my decision was right. Yes, my decision to go to the psychotherapist was right. I assured the doctor that it was alright. I went out of this session with a lot of benefits. Speech is not important, implementation is. Digging in the past will not be useful. You have to look at the future, Ahmed… You have to create the future…

but how? Should I search for Khaled to get out of this cursed circle?

I have to escape the circle of the past in order for me to flee from its prison. To run away from this blockade, I must encounter new experiences, whether good or bad. I have to look for new encounters at any cost.

I took my decision at this moment. I started the car; I traveled to Alexandria, wishing that my expectations would be right, and thus, find "Khaled". I wondered a lot while I was on the road, I noticed things I had never noticed before. I did not know these things but I felt strange on a road I had taken more than once, and saved its terrains by heart. By heart? This kind of rhetoric does not suit me. I felt alone on the road. I looked around me and did not find any car, I just heard their sound. This situation happened to me a lot lately. I looked at the side of the road and I noticed that someone was pointing at my direction; it was not Adel and not even Khaled, but it was rather Mohab.

He embarked on my car and I asked him what was he doing in such place, he explained that the car he was riding broke down. I wondered why there were no cars stopping at that place, I did not ask though!! I offered him help with my basic mechanic maintenance experiences, but he laughed and told me that he walked away from the car. I noticed that he tried to change the topic of our conversation. He asked me if I was searching for Khaled, I wondered again, how he knew that "Khaled" disappeared?! I asked him but he ignored my question and asked, "Do you think what is circling in your mind is true?" I was astonished for the third time and asked him: "Do you know what is in my mind?" He smiled a wry smile and asked me to focus on driving to avoid accidents.

I asked Mohab to come with me but he demanded to stay in the car, I went to the small room that was next to the stairs, I knocked on its door, the door was opened by a young man whom I did not know. I asked him about Bakr, he told me that he traveled to his hometown. There, he bought several acres and settled down. I asked him about Khaled, but he did not know him. It looked like my expectations were wrong. The unavailability of Bakr proved that my expectations were completely wrong. I expected that Bakr knew where Khaled was, but it seemed like Bakr was satisfied with the fortune he had accumulated from his profession and had become one of the property owners in his hometown.

I returned to the car, feeling irritated, but when I saw that Mohab had left the car, the feeling vanished. I looked around me and he was nowhere to be found. I did not search that much because I was tired and we were not playing hide and seek. It was not the suitable time for me to play. I decided to go back and think of another place Khaled may be at.

The sudden visit of Mohab sparkled my disorientation; why did he come? Why did he disappear? What did he benefit from what he did? He was not my friend. That was the second time I saw him. We would not be friends since we were different and I was not ready now for any new friendships. I'm already satisfied with what I have. Speaking of friendships, I should see Kareem again, as I have a feeling that he knew some information and he did not want to tell me about it. This was Kareem's habit ever since I knew him; he never says anything until the last moment.

I pushed through the road in record time. I looked at my watch; it was three in the morning and I had nothing to do. I was in a state that did not allow me to make any critical decision. It was difficult to go to Kareem now. I decided to go home to get some rest then I would go to him. I held the phone and called. When I was about to hang up, Kareem answered; his voice projected his feeling of sleepiness.

-"What is wrong, Ahmed?" He said it with a worried voice"

-"I have to see you."

-"ok, I will see you in the mosque after El Fajr Prayer."

Kareem puzzled me; his religious dealings were purely commercial transactions; he performed his religious duties and had no problem going to the Umrah each year. But, on the other hand, he had many western liberal views, which triggered our astonishment. He used to say; "the relationship between what is religiously allowed or prohibited is relative". In many occasions, he adhered to this logic to scrutinize particular mistakes. I did not want to say that Kareem was like his father, who used religion for financial gain. However, just like me, he needed much time to change for the better.

When I entered the mosque, I felt comfortable and I knew the reason. Long time had passed by since I entered that soothing place, which should have been my refuge in my ordeals, but I looked for other solutions.

It had been months since I last attended

Friday prayer. I justified my nonattendance by trivial pretexts. No, in fact, it was not trifling at all, it was terrifying to me that every Friday, the preacher talked about the torment of the grave; he artistically and meticulously described it and scared us with it. Instead of delineating the beauty of paradise, its eternity and greatness, he turned to the torment of the grave. He continually depicted how infidels, violators of human rights, mockers, and delinquent, would be tortured. I could have gone to another mosque but I took the easiest solution, so, I stopped going to the mosque. I wished someone would have entered my life to guide me, to direct me to the path of righteousness, but no one came.

I think that a subservient person resided inside me, or more precisely, a person who loved to be a subservient. In many occasions, Khaled steered both me and Adel, but the latter grew impatient of Khaled's behavior and convinced me to refuse the ideas of Khaled. Thus, I was once again steered to refuse. After reacting in such way, Khaled distanced himself from us for a while, but we managed attract him to us and we were once again together.

Inside each one of us there is a conscience that hurts us when we make a mistake. It might hurt us a lot when we make several blunders and it might not harm us when we continue making mistakes. Adel was an alive conscience to me and to Khaled, but he sometimes made the same mistakes with us. Occasionally, he would awaken me and help me announce my rebellion against Khalid. The death of Adel meant the bereavement of my living conscience, which was always by my side. Now the road is open-ended and none of us knows where to go.

I was engrossed in the abyss of my reflections; lost in my own line of thought. I woke up from these reflections by the end of the prayer. All what I knew was that my reflections had taken me away from the prayer; I was not doing anything but imitating worshipers like a child who went with his father to the mosque for the first time. I did not know why those obsessions were making me busy? Did they occupy entirely my life? All I wished for at that moment was for that story to end, it does not matter whether it ends in a good or bad way, what is important is for it to end.

Silence prevailed for moments. "I know where Khaled is, but he does not want anyone to know his whereabouts. Anyways, you have to be with him now." I was filled with hope. I and Khaled were on the same boat now. We could help each other overcome this catastrophic psychological situation.

-"Where?"

-"At the home of a respected Sheikh, I am his benefactor. His name is Sheikh Shamis. I will give you his address."

-"Why is he refusing to stay at home?"

-"he is upset; I thought it would be helpful to send him to Sheikh Shamis. I think he can guide him to the path of righteousness"

-"Is Sheikh Shamis the one whose [1]Fatwa you follow?"

He nodded his head positively; I said "Allah suffices me, for He is the best disposer of affairs".

On my way to the house, I tried to get rid of my fears. Eventually, my suspicions led me to the conclusion that Khaled had joined an extremist Islamic group, which fights the enemies of god and penalizes corrupted people of the world.

The smell of incense was spread all over the place. I sat upon a small sofa in a room that looked like a grave to me, Sheikh Shamis entered and in his hand was a cup of Talia. I asked him about Khaled, he told me that he did not want

---

1-Fatwa: is a term that refers to the opinion or well-read interpretation that is given by Mufti (an Islamic, well-informed scholar) on an issue related to Islamic law or the matters of Muslims

to meet anyone, I insisted on meeting him. He said," Ok, perhaps guidance will occur, absent consciences will finally be awakened, the hearts will be submissive to God, and the disease-affected hearts will lastly be purified, and I will guide you..." He was quiet for a while, conceivably looking for a word to end his modern verse. Laughingly, and at a time when I shouldn't have satirized, I said," Give me this gift". With askance, he looked at me; I was indifferent, all I cared about at that moment was meeting Khaled, even if this first encounter didn't go well.

My fears turned into reality when I saw Khaled wearing Jalabiya and holding a strange book which he was leafing through. When he realized I was there, he stood up and hugged me tightly while he was saying, "It is time for repentance and undertaking the path of righteousness, my friend".

I left Khaled's abode, feeling bad. Is this really the person whom I nicknamed strong sexual desire and whom I have known for years? Now he was talking to me about an immortal world and life and a mandatory martyrdom. He told me, "the most ideal solution now is for us to fight the corruption that people have fallen into and dragged us with them into." I did not answer. The reality was that he did not give time to answer. I would've preferred to talk with him about Adel. He did not talk about him as if he had forgotten about him or that he never existed. I wanted to go back to Kareem to ask him why he did this to Khaled. Why did he take him to this peculiar Sheikh? And how did he not get affected by this sheikh's extremist doctrines, although he had known him for a long time?

The insults of passersby, whom I almost hit, wake me up from my reflections. I arrived at the enormous shop of perfumes which was owned by Kareem's father.

Before I uttered anything related to the topic, he led me outside the shop.

-"let's go talk in the house."

Kareem closed the door of the room. He sat on a chair facing me as if he knew that we would converse for a while.

-"Why did you do that, Kareem?!"

- "It was the best solution; Khaled needed to be there at this particular period of his life and so do you."

-"Me too! You are free-willed, but you can't decide for people"

-"No, I am a red line, my father warned those people from coming close to me. They take a lot of money from my father as charity."

Silently, I stood up. I remembered that most of the discussions with Kareem were fruitless. I recalled the weird Sheikh with a scolding laugh. I left the house of Kareem, assured that I had lost all of my friends and that I was henceforth alone.

8

I started to feel like my head was empty, but at the same time, crazy ideas were crammed in it. What do I want? All I knew was that I was worn-out, tired of thinking of an unchangeable past and a future that seemed to be vague and to which I had no access. At this point, I was aware that I had been steered my entire life and I would continue to live as such. All I had to do was to wait for what would happen. I did not have to think about anything. Reflection is tiring for people who are in situation like mine. The line of my thought was cut by a call from Dalia. Her call at that time bewildered me. I looked at my watch; it was nine thirty. She told me that she was at the club, I asked her the reason why she was there at that time, she said that she was running and she told me she would tell me everything when I go to meet her. I did not argue with her a lot since I could not be more natural than I was.

I told her that I was coming right now. After I finished the call, I started crying. I was completely astonished by this sudden outburst of tears; I was not this sensitive before. The death of Adel had influenced me so much that whenever I recalled him, I cried. I cried in my life sometimes like any other normal human being. If my memory does not fail me, I cried three times and this was the fourth one. The second time was when uncle Kamal died, my situation was awful at that time and the death further worsened it. The first time was because of fear. The third time was because of Adel's death. I almost forgot my appointment with Dalia. I went hurriedly in order to be there on time.

We ran together and of course my fatigued shape only helped me run for a quarter of an hour, while Dalia was in a good shape and was able to continue running. I felt ashamed of myself. So, I held my stomach, pretending to have a stomachache. I looked at her eyes, they seemed worried. I assured her the ache was insignificant. She asked me to rest for a short while and I unhesitatingly agreed. We started to converse with each other. Our conversation revolved around Adel. After a period of time, Dalia draw my attention to a remark that distressed me; which was the fact that our conversation was centered on Adel, I told her that I knew that very well and I Loved talking about my friend, whom I would never forget whether we spoke about him or not. Dalia was quiet and she said after thinking for a short while; "I go to a psychotherapist, who advised me to forget the past and start a new future which I should build by myself." I smiled and told her that I was frequenting a psychotherapist as well and he instructed me to do the same thing. It looked like we are going to the same psychotherapist. She was surprised and said, "You look strong", I replied," I just pretend to be so, but deep inside, I feel an anguish that cannot be cured easily. Those who conceal their anguish inside suffer more than complainers" Ahmed, "you are perfect". I was taken aback by her words, for I am the last person in the world, who would be convinced to believe such words, I had always felt that I lacked something, a ganglion that cannot be solved since it grew with me, it became part and parcel of who I am.

When I saw Khaled for the first time, I felt that I was in need of something, Khaled was very straightforward, he did what he wanted to do and was never embarrassed of expressing his sexual desires freely; he would approach any girl; regardless whether she was a widow or divorcee.

I envied Adel when I had seen him with you. I wished I were in his place. I was happy when you disputed and I got even happier when you called him and he did not answer you. An inner injury would emerge in my being when you get back together. I held a grudge against Kareem because his father was rich and I wished we had exchanged roles; I became him and him me. Notwithstanding all this, all of my friends had their flaws. These flaws came to the surface as a result of the virtues that attracted me to them. Khaled, nicknamed strong desire, wouldn't venture to do anything unless he had satisfied his sexual impulses first. Adel was a very furious person; when he was outraged, nothing could stop him. There was another shortcoming that was more dangerous than being furious; after asking Adel or proposing a suggestion to him, he would accept it and then start thinking of a way to distract you from achieving what you want even after he had provided you with means to fulfill your suggestion.

Kareem had religious opinions that prohibited or allowed things; he didn't feel ashamed of receiving Fatwa from a mercenary Sheikh, who was unaware that if the inner self is virtuous, the outer self would be moral as well. Kareem, whose father owned men, who claimed to hold knowledge, but were only interested in money; they wanted to earn money. Kareem's father owned bank accounts, immensely gigantic buildings, towers that touched the clouds, and banks with altering economic benefits. He took part in projects with the sole aim of receiving financial gain from them. He never tasted failure; how could he lose? He was in charge of such projects and he was the one who accredited them.

What was all of that? What were all these abstracted thoughts that suddenly crossed my mind? I noticed that I haven't spoken for a while and that Dalia was bewilderingly looking at me. I was sure that all these internal reflections did not see daylight. I was also convinced that I didn't voice my inner reflections. I still haven't reached that condition yet; to say whatever came to my mind without thinking about it beforehand, people, who do this, are spontaneous, and I was undoubtedly not one of them.

"I will not be like Adel, Dalia". She was silent for a while before she responded; "I did not ask that, Ahmed. I want you as you are. Do not change or become another person. Just be yourself. That is what I want from you and I am not asking you for something impossible. I will not forget Adel and will not forget our days together but think of my situation, I am sick and your company makes me feel certain stability. Your presence in my life gives me hope in a future that reminds me of

Adel... Be next to me, please. Give me hope in this life".

"Dalia, I would like to help you but my presence in your life as a substitute of Adel is not useful. This is not to mention the fact that I have never had a relationship of this sort with a girl before and I'm afraid that it will fail since we are hasting matters." The last sentence I uttered was ironic, since the first part of it was a lie, given that I had many intimate relationships with women, while the second part was right, as I never had any intimate relationship with girls, but only with widows or divorcees. People who read this would presume that I had numerous relationships, but they were only three or four affairs, notable of them was my relationship with Madiha, which lasted for a while. All the other relationships ended quickly. Some of them were afraid of people's judgments in case they discovered about our affairs, others decided to end the affair in fear of the severe consequences it might yield.

What I meant was that I never wooed a girl into doing something that is incompatible with her morals. I had never been that clandestine lover for a wife who felt disgusted of a husband who did not clean his teeth before kissing her. Khaled preferred the obscene roles and it was one of his flaws, which sometimes compelled me to alienate myself from him.

"What haste are you talking about? We may be weak now but we are not rushing things. We need a decision. That is all what we need, Ahmed, a decision which will determine both my destiny and yours" said Dalia.

"You said it yourself; Dalia, we are weak, hastiness is an outcome of weakness. You know that weak people take haste decisions and this feebleness is a byproduct of fear. Fear is the third outcome of feebleness and rashness. All this generates a triangle whose three edges are fragility, hastiness, and fear"

"We are not in a class of mathematics, Ahmed. The situation cannot be delayed. I am sure if Adel was still alive and saw me, he would have done anything I asked for at any cost. You know, when I was running at the gym, I wished the "track" would never end, that I would keep on running until the end of the world. I wished I would keep running until I fell apart and all the nightmares, which overwhelmed my soul, vanish. I'm worn-out; I feel unstable. I wish I become who I was in the past, Ahmed. You understand what I want"

The situation was truly unbearable. Dalia's state was worsening before my eyes; she might even be threatening to commit suicide. I had to put up with her until her condition improved or at least until I consulted my psychotherapist. I was incapable of making any decision at that moment.

When I looked at Dalia, I noted that her condition was really deteriorating and I had to save her. At that moment, the expression "Okay" came out of my lips. A hopeful smile was drawn on her face; I comforted her and promised that I would always be there for her whenever she needed me.

I went back home, I was so tired that I slept without changing my clothes. I saw numerous dreams that night that were probably caused by the tranquilizers I had been taking. The imaginary scenes in my subconscious mind needed to see daylight, but what daylight in the underworld, which I plunged into every time my eyes were closed. I heard the voices of Adel, Dalia, Kareem, Mohab, Khaled and Madiha. I could see my parents from afar; running towards my direction. They bumped into me; they even went over me as if I didn't exist, like I was ashes of a fire that had been extinguished.

I suddenly woke up, incapable of realizing what I had seen, I needed some time to reconcile

Meccano

with myself. I remembered the incomplete dream that I had seen before. My life was like a Meccano toy. I was like a little child who was unaware of what he was doing; he played with the game and created an odd shape. He separated the parts of the shape from each other and tried to join them together, but couldn't do so. Again, he tried but in vain. The child felt bored and left the shape incomplete. Ghosts came, disassembled the pieces, and reconstructed them; they took to pieces the small robot child and restructured it once again. The ghosts were woofing and howling while they were immersed in pulling me into pieces and remaking me. It was like a vision, a dream I saw, but tried to overlook with the hope of crafting it in the oblivion of my consciousness.

I left the bed lazily; it was probably an offshoot of the exhaustion that stroke me shortly before what happened to Adel. I thought about the situation for a while. Adel passed away, Khaled was lost, and Kareem was not honest with me; he thought that he was mending a situation which the three of us had ruined. He assumed that god was taking revenge on us for the w r o n g things we did during our short lifetimes.

Dalia was like me; suffering from psychological disorders and our conditions were getting worse with each passing minute. I wish I could take part in fixing this situation. "The lame may enter first", a proverb my mother used to tell me to encourage me, at times when I felt crippled.

I spent the remainder of the day in artificial tranquility. I felt a severe headache; I fetched for medicine and I found the pills that Anya offered me during her stay in Egypt. I checked the expiration date; it was consumable since it wouldn't expire until 4 months from now. I took a pill, but I felt no improvement. Then, I took another one, and I felt relaxed and slept.

My parents disappeared and came back from afar; I heard voices of people, whom I knew, drawing closer to me. I recognized the owners of these voices when they approached me. They formed a circle around me. When my father tried to penetrate the circle, they clutched each other's hands tightly. I tried to reach my father but in vain, I felt panic and dread devastating me.

The following day, I woke up early. I thought extensively about why I didn't visit Adel's grave. I still haven't lost my senses yet, but the idea of visiting his grave was always present in my mind ever since he passed away.

I sat next to Adel's grave. I tried to prevent myself from crying, but I couldn't; I sobbed bitterly as if it was the first I have ever cried. The sound of my groans was so high that I thought they reached the sky. My stay there lasted for the whole day, the sun departed and darkness prevailed. I did not expect that time would pass by as quickly as it did. I got up and I heard a familiar voice; it was Mohab's; "it's too late to visit Adel". Strange, I thought that Mohab did not know Adel or maybe Khaled told him. I convinced myself with this explanation, although I knew that Khaled and Mohab were not friends. They only sat together for virtually half an hour and I saw Mohab on two occasions. The first one was when he was sitting with Khaled and the second time was while I was looking for Khaled.

"Why are not you answering? Are you searching for an answer? You forgot Adel and you no longer care about him? Excuse me, you are not alone; Khaled forgot Adel as well. It looks like you were not true friends."

I mockingly smiled, I gave him my back, facing Adel's grave. "I will never forget Adel, he was my faithful friend."

"That explains what you are doing with his girlfriend, Dalia. The effect of your friendship with him is clear now. Oh I believe you! Stop acting, you are not sad because of Adel's bereavement, you are pretending to be sad to win the heart of Dalia"

"You know Dalia as well. It is obvious that you do not know anything. You only know names, but I would like to ask you, what do you want from me?"

"It's late now. Are you going to leave or stay here? I got to warn you that if you sleep among these graves, your dreams will be more dreadful than they already are."

"Why are you ignoring me? From where do you know all this information about me? How do you know Dalia? The most startling thing of all is that you know about my unfinished dreams, and more precisely, my incomplete dreams. How do you know about this?"

No one answered my questions; I looked behind me and did not find him. At this moment, I felt scared. I ran as fast as I could. I fell and got up quickly to continue running to stay away from the graves.

It was clear that Mohab was stalking me. I had to know the reason why he was closely stalking me and how come he knew about my deficient dreams. I was not in a horror or science fiction movie, in life, everything followed certain logic and calculations. If so, what was happening to me? It was abnormal and it inspired anxiety and fear within me. Although I visited Adel's grave, I didn't feel relieved. I hope that I would attain psychological stability and relaxation, but my visit to Adel's grave was more like a duty and it didn't feel right. I decided to go the following day for two reasons: the first one was to get this psychological stability which had lost its way before reaching me... And the second one was that I wanted to see Mohab. I wish I could see him, I wish I could know all the details. I wouldn't leave unless I knew what I want.

Desperately, I waited for three hours; neither Mohab nor emotional relief showed up. I decided to go back home since I felt a combination of fear, boredom, and confusion, a sensation I have never encountered before. I promptly changed my mind and decided to stay for half an hour.

My father was trying to penetrate the cursed circle to reach me but they sealed it very tightly. I could not move and felt like I was paralyzed, though I could stand on my place. The countenances began to fade away, and so were the facial features of people, only bodies could be perceived. The circle was narrowing down. My mother was crying and screaming, while my father tried desperately to reach me and I couldn't move.

I woke up; feeling frightened. The dream this time was longer than before and with more accurate details. I decided to leave immediately and go back home since I didn't want my psychological condition to deteriorate. I was obliged to stay home until my next appointment with my psychotherapist.

Time was slowly passing or that was how I felt. I lost the ability to sense time. Before, I took advantage of every minute of my time, but now I only moved for few minutes. I felt like my body was in a state of spasm and my muscles were drained. I thought of doing something to escape this disheartening atmosphere. So, I wore my clothes and went out.

Yasser lived in this place, according to his account. I knocked on the door given that the doorbell was not functioning. Yasser's mother opened the door for me. I reminded her of myself, she invited me into the house, I asked her about Yasser and she told me he was playing soccer in the street. I asked for her permission to go check on him, but she refused and said; "He is good now and the proof is that he went to play soccer" I insisted on seeing him. Signs of annoyance could be seen on her face. She went to the window and called loudly a little kid, named Mohamed, and told him to call Yasser who was playing soccer in a nearby street.

Yasser greeted me warmly. He seemed tired. He told me he played with his friends every day for two consecutive hours. We talked for a while and it was obvious that he was passionate about soccer. I asked him if he was playing in any club, but his face showed signs of sadness, he told me that his lifetime wish was to play for Al Ahly football team.

"Oh.. Al Ahly from the very beginning! Why do you not try to start playing for a small club? Then, try to prove yourself and be worthy of what you achieve"

"I tried but I failed. I went with my father to a club that plays in the second league division and they did not accept me. I must have contacts to be accepted"

"Really, even a club that plays in the second league division, maybe you do not know how to play."

"No, not at all, I'm like many of the friends, all we need is contacts to be accepted"

I was silent for few moments. Then, I told him that I would try to help. His mother looked at me suspiciously; I gazed quickly at her worried eyes. Was this crazy woman thinking that I would kidnap her son? I looked again at Yasser and noted that happiness had engulfed his countenances. He asked me to promise that I would help him. I promised him, but my offer to assist him was only a way of reviving hope within him.

I enjoyed the time I spent with Yasser. Like any other kid of his age, Yasser was pure; still haven't been contaminated by the filth of life. I remembered when I was his age, I was a hard working student and successful in my studies. I did not have any hobbies, except for studying. I was the first in my class for three years in a row. Last time I was first was in the third grade. Back then, I had no friends. I recalled an accident that had happened to me after the examination results were revealed in the third grade. At that day, I saw in the eyes of Walid, who was ranked in the second place after me, something which I didn't know back-then.

The school honored me along with the outstanding students of the school; I hurriedly went to the house because I wanted my mother to see the fruits of her efforts with me. That day, Walid followed me along with a dog, I didn't know where he brought that dog from. After a while I heard him calling me, I looked behind me and saw that Walid was pointing at me and then urged the dog to go after me. I ran as fast as I could but the dog was faster than me, I played with him the game of the cat and mouse. He disappeared behind some cars but this silly dog was able to find me. So, I ran again. I was surprised by the dog's persistence to chase after me; it was as if we were enemies. I stood, my back leaned against the wall, and felt tears as they poured from my eyes unwillingly.

That was the first time I have ever cried. The dog stood there, barking at me. It had performed its duty successfully; it managed to incite within me a feeling of terror and blockaded me in that corner. I remembered that I received all kinds of physical and verbal assaults from Walid. I was paralyzed; unable to defend myself. I learned that day the meaning of hatred and how sometimes humans are controlled by the desire to take revenge. This accident left the second deepest scars in me.

The following year, when I got my friends, I wanted to use that to take revenge, I asked them to help me teach him a lesson, they agreed, but after that, Adel refused completely and asked us not to hurt Walid, since we would make the mistake, which Walid made, when he let jealousy took over him. Adel told me to forget about it. Although I obeyed the commands of Adel, I felt, at that moment, that justice was not served. I still have that desire to confront Walid and physically assault him until I feel satisfied.

I did not know why I remembered that situation now; I didn't want helplessness and inability to take over Walid's soul. Perhaps fate placed me on his way so that I could help him. He took my cellphone number and he told me that he was going to call me to remind me of my promise. I did not hesitate and gave him my number. Dalia called me; she told me that she ran every day at the club. She invited me to exercise with her and I welcomed that idea.

What I feared the most happened; I only ran for fifteen minutes and then stopped to rest due to my weakening shape. I told her if I was a burden on her exercises, I would not come again, but she was upset because of my words and said, "I am worried about our psyches" Her psychotherapist told her that exercising was very important in improving her psychological status. Our conversation was halted by the voice of a fight. When I asked Dalia about the reason, she said that fights were common at the gym, since a lot of visitors of the club wanted to use the playground, but they were denied access to it because the playground was exclusively reserved for members of the club. I was taken aback since for a while I had been frequenting the gym with Adel or Kareem, but never used any of the facilities of the gym since we were not in a good shape to do.

I asked her why I was allowed into a place which I'm not authorized to be at .She laughed and I noticed this time that her laugh was as pure as the tones of a sad guitar, I didn't know where I heard such words, maybe on one of the boring programs of TV. She told me that her father was a lawyer and he was a member of administration board of the club. Moreover, she was the best tennis player at the club. She also represented the club in many Tennis national championships. But she did not travel outside to represent it because she feared planes. When she told me all of that, I remembered Yasser. I asked her to use her contacts to get Yasser into the soccer club. She accepted my request without hesitation. I wondered why she did not ask me about whether he was skilled or not. I talked to her about my concern, she said she was going to put him at the beginning of the road and he had to continue by himself. If he is talented, he would become one of the most important players on the junior soccer team. If he is not skilled, then that means she did what she had to do and she responded to my request. I thanked her so much. I called Yasser and told him to come with his father now to the club, and he was extremely happy. Dalia called the coach who was still sleeping in his house. After an hour and half, Yasser received his team uniform, his sport shoes, and a club card that gives him permission to enter the club at training days. The trainer gave him some instructions then left. Yasser thanked me so much and his father looked at me gratefully and smiled; "you know Yasser's mother warned us from coming here... I do not know why she is scared of you. She said you only bring misfortunes" I laughed so much at this sentence, his father apologized and explained that he was not intending to offend me, but he was just quoting what his wife said without any change. She has the right to worry about her son. Moreover, we met in some distressing circumstances. So, it's okay if she was worried .I left Yasser who was about to cry, a cry of happiness.

Dalia was ecstatic as well. She explained that she was happy because she fulfilled my wish and made Yasser contented. I left her after we had agreed to run tomorrow. My spirits were touching the sky at that moment... I forgot all my problems when I helped Yasser. I even thought of doing some voluntary work for some charity organization.

Before leaving, I asked Dalia about the timing of her training sessions and those of Yasser. She enumerated the schedule for me .I decided to attend some of Dalia's and Yasser's training sessions. I thought that I should be close to him, because I believed that he would help me improve my psychological state and his company would ease my healing.

I was astonished by the hastiness with which the events had advanced. Yesterday, Yasser asked me to help him and today I really helped him. This universe is strange. Our life is sometimes crowded by events, while at other times we hardly find anything to do. There are boring occasions when time passes slowly, like when we are waiting for sleep to come, or are just waiting in general. Time goes by slowly in minutes of failure or disagreeable moments. How annoying it is!

All I wished for was to regain my psychological stability whatever it costs. I was astonished by the fact that I find excuse for everything I had done.

Until now, I never did anything wrong to Adel. But I did not want my words to be my passport to pass to the world of blunders. Adel was like my brother, In fact, he was really my brother; a brother whom my mother never gave birth to. I lived alone in this life until I found my friends, but they left me now. I did not know who should be blamed for this; us or the life that offered us only few choices to choose from. Throughout my lifetime, multiple choices questions constituted a psychological burden to me given that I thought that there was more than just one answer and it was not listed in the choices. It was like a very narrow hole made by a needle.

I used to study hard for the exams, but I sadly forgot a lot shortly afterwards. I didn't suffer from the syndrome of forgetting since the early days of childhood. It was not until I enrolled in high school that I started to forget. This negatively influenced my performance in school. The four of us had uneven levels. Khaled joined commerce school, Adel opted for economics in college, Kareem signed up for a private school to study engineering, and Ahmed joined law school. I felt the reemergence of the complex of inferiority in my psyche, it never left me. After I was the most successful for a while amongst them, I became the least successful. I believed that this was one of the factors that impacted my psyche harmfully. For this reason, I sometimes alienated myself from them, most probably because I envied them from time to time.

9

It was the worst vacation I have ever had; I did not like mid-term vacation. It was neither short-termed like holidays of religious feasts, nor long-termed like the vacations of the end of the school year. I decided to throw away all what happened behind me so that I would enter the second semester with enough strength, although the latest unfortunate incidents drained my potency.

When school started, I managed to strike a balance between going to college and watching the training of Yasser and Dalia as well as corresponding with Anya and attending sessions with my psychotherapist. Thank God nothing happened to this moment that would annoy me.

I believed in the signs of the divine and I liked their emergence in my life. When a person prayed for me or pleaded God to grant me luck, I was sure that the prayer would someway help me out. I recalled this topic because yesterday I used the metro since my car broke down; I sat next to an old man. Moments passed by before he looked at me and said," My wife died a week ago. Recite for her El Fatiha, please." With an unheard tone, I recited the Quranic chapter. I felt that I made a mistake. So, I read it repeatedly till I was sure that I recited it correctly. Then, my hands skimmed through my face, implying that I finished reciting Al Fatiha.

I have never seen before a man who hated his son. "I went abroad to work there. I sent them money regularly to ensure that they have a decent life. When I came back to my home, I found out that my son had become accustomed to my absence and neither cared about me nor respected me, he was only interested in my money; He took a lot from me and squandered it on disastrous projects. When he misspent my money, he stole his mother's money. She was intending to use the money to go on pilgrimage. Out of grieve, she died. I sold the apartment and went on pilgrimage twice, once for me and another one for her. I live now at my sister's house and I go every day to my wife's grave to spend some time with her and read Quran for her. Allah suffices me, for He is the best disposer of affairs" He repeated this hysterically until he stood up from his seat and left the metro.

I did not know why I felt that this message was addressed to me, perhaps it was because I neglected Adel. The last time I went there was to see Mohab, but he didn't show up.

I read El Fatiha for Adel and I sat next to his grave reciting verses from the Quran. I felt comfortable and it boosted my spirits. I decided to go and visit Adel every day, sit with him for some time so I would not feel that I abandoned him.

I visited Adel's grave regularly and I even added these visits to my daily routine. I started memorizing a new Quranic verse every day. I wondered why Dalia did not visit Adel. Dalia became a huge mystery to me. How come she loved Adel and still got bothered whenever we talked about him. Her psyche would be weary on the mention of his name. Thus, I avoided talking about him in her presence. With time, I, too, forgot about him until the man, whose name I didn't know, reminded me of him.

Adel stood between me and Dalia; I could not determine the nature of the relationship that tied us together.

My mother was still crying and my father was trying to breakthrough that barrier but he could not. Dalia appeared from far away; she came closer and went through the circle, like a transparent light. When I looked at the countenances of people, I noticed that they were omitted. Dalia came closer, stretched her arms to embrace me. The circle widened again, yet, it remained impenetrable.

I woke up to the sound of my alarm clock. It was five o'clock. It was time for me to go. I had an issue; Dalia had an important match after an hour from that moment. I did not know where to go? I decided to go to Adel; I thought that he needed me next to him more than Dalia. He would be comfortable and sure that I did not betray him and would never do. I talked with Adel for a little bit then I read him some Quran.

My phone rang; Dalia was crying because she was defeated in the match. It was the first match she lost in a while. She got beaten because of me, because I was not present in the game, she said. I calmed her down and told her that I was coming right away.

She was in a bad state. I wished time would go back; I would have gone to the club, stood next to her and encouraged her during the match. When I told her that her cries hurt my heart, she regained her composure. Her coach was surprised that she was defeated by a beginner .This defeat almost prevented her from representing her club in the national championship of Tennis. But the coach decided to give Dalia a second chance by organizing another match for her.

I attended the game and supported Dalia enthusiastically. She won the match in record time and I understood the rules of the game. She told me it was the best match she has ever played in her entire life. I did not know why I felt at that moment that Dalia needed me more than Adel? It was the first time I didn't visit Adel. I felt guilty because of what I did and I promised that I would never stop visiting Adel regardless of the circumstances.

I visited Adel's grave daily; I even paid him visits during the period of exams. I forgot about Khaled, Mohab and Kareem, or that was what I thought. Summer vacation started and so did the national championship of Tennis. I was busy supporting Dalia in the tournament. I supported her match after another till she won the championship, as it was expected. We celebrated together as she used to do with Adel .I did not do it to imitate him but because she asked me to do that.

Yasser was making notable progress meanwhile; he told me that the coach liked his skills a lot. Hence, I was contented because I was the reason why he was happy.

Psychotherapy sessions ensued one after the other. I was in a good state; I told my psychotherapist a lot of things but concealed many others, probably because I was afraid of looking weak. What was important now was that I became better and surpassed that silly stage, a stage which I would never remember again. The only thing that tied me with that stage was my Friday visits to Adel's grave. I only did that to look faithful in his eyes. The doctor prescribed some tranquilizers to me. I asked him whether my condition would worsen again or not. He said, mostly no. His answer did not satisfy me though.

I feared that if I continued to be scared of going to my former deteriorating state, the disease might come back.

Dalia was exactly like me, she, too, had been cured and had regained her strength. She seemed like a flower that blossomed. Her laugh seemed more beautiful and purer. I was assured that we were feeling great and that our spirits were high.

It was no surprise that Dalia was selected to represent Egypt in the international championship of Tennis, since her level had improved significantly. I encouraged her a lot to travel but she was scared at the beginning then she was convinced that she could participate and achieve grand results. Moreover, I convinced her that her phobia of travelling by plane was not going to prevent her. I explained that I would support her and if she did not want to participate in the international championships for herself, she could do it for me.

Everything was arranged quickly. Dalia traveled. Everything was going smoothly. For this reason, I became more optimistic. I promised to call her daily as I was sure that it would encourage her to win or at least represent Egypt in an honorable way, since it was her first time to ever participate in an international competition.

If things continued going this way, I would never feel fatigued again as I did previously. No, No... I did not want to experience what I encountered in the past. I would not feel good. What was important now was to encourage Dalia and Yasser as I saw myself in them and considered their success to be my success. I knew this might sound negative or an invitation to laziness and stagnation, but it was the truth; I had nothing to do for the time being; I neither had a project to accomplish nor a dream to fulfill. All I owned now was some encouragement which made me stand behind the doer of victory. It gave me the right to celebrate with him, feel a sensation of self-achievement as well as self-satisfaction, and reconcile with myself, a self that exhausted and tortured me and inflected me with diseases, which I had nothing to do, except the fact that I followed the lead of others and had no choice. Or more accurately, I had a choice but I picked the wrong one.

Why did I revert to this boring sad rhyme again? Yes, I had many opportunities but I didn't seize any of them, what happened? Did the universe explode? The doctor told me that I shouldn't dig into the past or my former decisions. What else? Ha?! Cleaning is a civilized behavior, squandering water is wrong because they are going to steal the river, and quality is a prerequisite in the culture of competition. My school is developed but the centers are much better. Studying hard means passing the exams, cheating would ensure that you get high marks. I liked my disgusting jokes so I chuckled so much because of them. I remembered teachers repeating outdated slogans without understanding. The outmoded slogans were like idols. Teachers found their fathers and forefathers repeating the same slogans. Hence, they did the same. At any rate, this was not the proper time to be talking about silly teachers, who used to put glasses on their noses in a provocative manner. As it is the costume in my country, people are not interested in the regulations. In fact, people are afraid of many things in life, but the law is certainly not one of them.

I tried changing the line of my thought. I returned to thinking of Yasser and Dalia. I reflected upon my self-fulfillment and how it was closely tied to the prospective achievement of Dalia. I became like a girl, who cannot wait to get married, so she could have kids, who would allegedly make her feel satisfied with herself. I felt sad that I played this role; I had to find something to achieve for myself, not with the achievements of others, but with my own, I have to discover a field where I can find myself so that my life would be prosperous like I wished it to be, and nothing would lead me astray from the life I always wanted to have .But what do I want?!

People, who observe you from afar, utter some prejudices about you. I always spoke little because I feared the judgments of people, but even so, their judgments were severe; people looked at me as an introvert. Adel was the person who guided me; he always encouraged me not to be shy. Indeed, I no longer feared the judgments of people and I reached a balanced state of mind.

I reckoned that Adel's self-confidence

stemmed from Dalia, while my temporary self-confidence emanated from the presence of Anya in my life. The strange thing was that although Dalia was with me now, I still haven't entirely regained my self-confidence. That was why I insisted on achieving a project of my own so that I wouldn't need Yasser or Dalia anymore, and I wouldn't feel fatigued , like I felt when I lost Adel. The rule says that you must anticipate the loss of something just because you love it.

I was astonished that I did the same activities I performed when Dalia was around me; I recurrently ran in the club and I grew fond of it now. I was no longer getting tired after a short period of time; I believed the improvement in my health was a byproduct of the recovery of my psyche. I wished things would go in a slow pace, I did not want earsplitting tones or unexpected incidents; I needed forethought; I needed to restructure things, it was time to take a decision in regard to my relationship with Dalia or start a new successful project or do other things which were not in my head now.

I grew the habit of reading; a habit I learned from Dalia. My doctor encouraged me to read too. I never had any keen interest in reading; I only read textbooks. At the outset, my eyes were caught by whatever I saw, but gradually my preferences became more accurate. I'm not a fan of books that contained a lot pages, I preferred articles and short stories, but Dalia told me that was just the start ,and after a while, and when I grew accustomed to reading, I would enter the next stage; the stage of novels, literature books, translations.. I did not ask her what was after that, so that I would not feel depressed.

I was astounded by the long-termed plans which Dalia set for herself and wanted to set for me, I loved spending my day like a normal worker, who only thinks about how his day is going to end and never reckons about the future, but Dalia liked to think about upcoming years like business men or bankers. I did not know why these two specific categories crossed my mind.

The difference between me and Dalia lied in our past. Our experiences and expertise shape our vision of life. Debts that pile up from the past and which we never take into consideration, a line of thought in which we are engrossed and never manage to escape. We all live in a micro world of our own; it affects us our decisions and choices just like our environment shaped our personality when we were children. Our personality traits are determined by the environment wherein we live and they are engraved in us; no one can ever change them. Even if someone did alter them, it would be momentary and eventually things would go to the way they were.

I spent the rest of my day watching television. The time passed by quickly, I slept early that day, I set my alarm since tomorrow was Friday and I would visit Adel's grave. My duty towards Adel was to always keep him in my mind and never let anything whatsoever distract me from visiting him.

Adel was waiting for me, although he hated waiting and he never came on time. Now, he waited eagerly for our meeting and so did I. I longed for our meetings because they purified my mind and soul, and helped me go through the upcoming days with an air of sincere calmness and optimism. How happy I was!!!

10

The first day I spent without Dalia was characterized by tranquility, I wished things would continue going like this. The noisy doorbell rang at midnight, who would come at this time? I slept early because I no longer had any friends. I got up quickly to see who was ringing the bell, I looked through the peephole of the door, and I could not identify the features of the person behind the door. So, I opened it; It was the last person I expected to see; Mohab.

After exchanging some superfluous civil utterances, I asked Mohab about the reason behind his visit at this late hour of night, but he ignored my inquiry and started talking non-stop about friendship, the duties of friends towards each other, and other things of that sort. I asked him why he was addressing me in particular, since I knew very well what he was saying and I never betrayed a friend of mine in my entire life.

"Adel.. You betrayed Adel and you do not want to admit that, can you tell me what the nature of your relationship with Dalia is?"

"A very normal relationship, we are friends; living in a society that does not understand such kind of friendships, but why are you intruding into my personal life. Your intrusion is irritating me."

"I was trying to help you get out of your ordeal, but now you are not appreciating my favor."

"How were you helping me when you disappeared whilst I was healing and now you emerged again?"

"It is clear; you do not appreciate what I had done for you. I stayed away from you so that you can forget about the past and commence a new life."

"You were not my only connection with the past; there was Adel, Kareem and Khaled."

"Adel died. If you think of something else other than that, then you are still sick. Kareem gave up on you, and as for Khaled, you know his destiny. Then, who is left? No one is left but me. When I disappeared, you lose your connection with the past, and thus, you were cured"

"You sound like psychotherapists. What is your job?"

"A director and before you ask about more details I am going to tell you. I directed a lot of movies which were banned for more than one reason. I made documentary movies and they too were banned for more than one reason, and before you ask again for more details, my movies were banned for moral or ethical purposes. There were horror movies that contained scenes which were not suitable for people with weak hearts"

"If all your movies were banned, why are you still working in this profession? How do you provide for yourself? I have many questions about your mysterious character and I need to learn about them"

"Do not bother yourself as you will not find anything, I will answer all your questions at the right time. Now I will answer only one question, which is the reason behind this sudden visit, I know that you feel lonely after Dalia traveled. That's why I came."

"You know Dalia traveled, your information is very up-to-date. Where did you get all these accurate details from? We will not speak till you answer all my questions."

"Haven't I just told you that I am a director? In order to flourish in this profession, you must have precision and an exceptional power of observation Anyways, I will leave you now to get some rest, since I know that you were sleeping. We will meet tomorrow"

Mohab went to the door and departed, leaving me thinking and having doubts about this night visit, a visit I learned nothing from, but only reminded of small forgotten bits of my past. At any rate, Mohab might not come again and that would be to my advantage. That's the last thought that crossed my mind before I slept.

When I woke up, I thought that Mohab's visit was just a dream, but when I leafed through the events of the previous night, I assured myself that Mohab was real, not an offshoot of my imagination.

When Adel and I lost control once, Khaled left us for a while. During that period, he got to know a group of boys. Khaled told me that Mohab was not one of the members of that group. This group made Mohab's acquaintance later. They liked his mysterious nature and style. Khaled's group was composed of three individuals; Khaled, Amir and Mofek. When Khaled introduced me to them, I sympathized with Amir who had a disfigured face. His face was split into two halves; one was thrilling, full of vivacity and vitality, while the other half was dim and miserable as if it was a dead person's face. Mofek was very ordinary, like any other commoner. I was surprised that Khaled got to know them, since they were different from him in everything; namely their way of thinking and character.

To break the boredom that devastates our lives, sometimes, we, humans, tend to meet new people without paying special attention to their personalities or getting to know them very well. I thought that Amir and Mofek were at this stage of life when they met Mohab and Khaled. Maybe what attracted me to Khaled fascinated them too. As for Mohab, he may easily amaze you with the information he knows about you. He would make you feel like you are special. Moreover, his mysterious nature and the little information he offered about himself attracted people to him. Curiosity is a silly thing after all. My thoughts were cut by another contemplation, I did not know where the idea was. I didn't know where Amir and Mofek were. Learning from people's mistakes was one of the most important lessons I learned from reading, a habit which Dalia guided me to.

I went to the coffee shop where Khaled and his friends used to go. When I asked the worker there about them, he told me that they were permanent customers, but they stopped coming for a long time. I asked him about their addresses, but he mocked me and said that he was not accustomed to writing down the addresses of his customers. He said he was not the mayor of the neighborhood. I left him. After slightly walking away from him, I called him and gave him an offensive hand gesture, spit on the floor and ran away. I loved doing some childish acts once in a while. This action had nothing to do with my cure, and thus, I didn't tell my psychotherapist about it, since I thought it was insignificant.

I considered asking the shops, which were near the café, about Amir, the boy with the disfigured face. . Amir lived near these shops. So, I figured that he might have frequented them; it is human nature to hang around places that are near them, since it makes them feel secure. I asked people there, but the answers were always negative. I went to other people and asked, but once again, no one gave me a satisfactory answer. I went back home feeling disheartened because of that.

My mind was occupied by ideas of the disappearance of Amir and Mofek. I reckoned about another consideration; perhaps they lived far away from the place where they used to meet Mohab and Khaled. They were probably bored by the routine of life and decided to look for something new. I cursed the stupidity that made Amir and Mofek, with their peaceful, stable personalities, be acquainted with Khaled and Mohab. Maybe they weren't stable or tranquil.

After all, what do I know about them? This disappearance raised my suspicions; perhaps something really bad happened to them.

If I asked Mohab, he would most likely ignore my inquiry and start talking about a different topic, as was his habit. His negligence made me feel like I was the last person he would speak to, but strangely enough, he knew a lot of information about me. It felt like it was a bizarre paradox.

I reckoned that Mohab wouldn't tell me anything. But anyways, I had to penetrate the secrecy and mysteriousness that surrounded Mo.. Mo..Mohab..Mohab.. At least, I was sure of his name, I only had to know more information about him so I would know to whom I was talking.

I was ready to meet Mohab at any moment; I knew that he deliberately met me in sudden incidents. What if I made up some impulsive incident and forced him to come, I had to do something strange to force him to come, but where from? I thought he was watching me! And if he did, why was he stalking to me in particular? And how did this imperceptible surveillance happen?

I walked in the street, but I didn't feel like I was being watched by anyone. I purposely looked behind me and scrutinized the faces of passersbys.

Yet, I did not find what I was looking for. I walked in the streets; following the rules of surveillance evasion; I did not walk in a long street, I changed my ways continually, took subsidiary roads and I constantly looked around me.

I had no new ideas in my mind. I only had biding thoughts that needed to be turned into actions by someone, so that I, as usual, react.

I finally came up with an idea that would draw the attention of Mohab to me and force him to meet me, but how would he find me because I was sure he was not stalking me. I sat by the side of the café, so that the worker there wouldn't see me and punish me for what I had done to him earlier. For an hour, nothing new happened, I felt bored. I hence decided to leave, but at that very moment, a person tapped my shoulder and sat next me.

How did you know my place? I repeated that question hysterically. Mohab was trying to say something, but I did not give him the chance to do so. I repeated my question without listening to what he was saying. He remained silent till I stopped.

"Are you done? You are not being watched, why would I stalk you anyways? I have a lot of things to do, things which are more important than stalking you. I think, you think, so we convene at a meeting point, it is not important where this meeting point is, what is more essential is that we have a mutual point. It is sort of telepathic communication or rational reasoning, both of which lead to the same results, do you understand me?"

"Do you think my reasoning is logical?"

"Yes, very rational. You recalled Amir and Mofek since you want to know what had happened to them. I will tell you what I know about them; ever since Khaled left them and went back to you and Adel, I never visited them again"

I said mockingly, "You follow Khaled wherever he goes, are you his consort?"

"Let's leave this place", he responded, ignoring my question.

I went back home with Mohab, we sat down and talked for few moments about life. The conversation was tedious. After I expressed my dissatisfaction with the chat, he left. Mohab opened the door and departed. A wild idea crossed my mind at that moment; to follow Mohab. I descended the stairs quickly after him. I arrived at the street, looked to my right and left, but he was nowhere to be found. I was determined to do this again in his next visit to my house.

Time passed by, Mohab did not appear, tomorrow would be Friday, my weekly meeting with Adel. I always talked to Dalia and encouraged her to continue doing her best, as she usually did. She promised me not to come back without winning the trophy.

Yasser was taking his training seriously; I attended some of his morning training sessions and supported him. What was really annoying me was Sherief, who was one year older than Yasser and trained with him. I noticed that he envied Yasser. He told me about him before; he explained to me that Sherief continually said that Yasser was not worthy of training with the club, since he was not a member in it. Moreover, Yasser told me that Sherief was always inclined to tackle him aggressively whenever he had the ball. I advised Yasser not to care about him and to regard that hostility as a motive to be the greatest in the team; he nodded his head in agreement.

My parents called; they would be here in approximately one week. They always came at this time of year. They are engineers in one of the largest companies in the field of communication; they are granted one month and a half as their annual leave.

I became so accustomed to their absence in my life that their presence became a burden on my shoulders. In ordinary days, I was not restrained by commitments to anyone. However, with their company, I felt restricted; I was like a fish caught in the trap of a ruthless fisherman. I always felt paralyzed and unable to act freely when my father was in Egypt or while I was studying in college, which represented a huge problem to me ever since it started. In such days, I would spend most of my time at home and I wouldn't move unless I was going to college or the bathroom.

Mohab called me and told me; "I have found what you need". I understood from his speech that he had found Amir and Mofek. I demanded to meet them promptly, but he refused, saying that he had set up a meeting with them on the next day at 8 o'clock in the morning. I wondered at the suspicious timing of our gathering; who would meet anyone at 8 o'clock in the morning? Mohab noted that it was their condition to meet us at such an hour. Thus, I accepted it although I had suspicions. My doubts soon disappeared and were replaced by thoughts about the following day's meeting at 8 o'clock at my place.

Mohab warned me;" Don't worry if I'm late". When the call ended, I recalled that the following day was a special day to me; it was the day of my visit to Adel's grave. I promised him that I would never stop frequenting his grave.

I slept that night, hoping that I would woke up with a decision at my disposal.

Dalia hugged me tightly, as the circle widened. The countenances of those with no features bore the features of Adel. An expression of displeasure was drawn on the face of Adel for few moments. Then, it disappeared.

With irritation, I woke up; I had no desire whatsoever to continue having that dream. Although the dream was not as terrifying as those before it, but I reckoned that I was watching the same series of dreams, dreams that exacerbated my life.

I took my decision, wore my clothes, and went towards the door in hesitation till my hand reached the door knob. I grasped it strongly, like a drowning man who was clutching at his survival rope. I moved the door knob in a feeble way, a manner that didn't correspond with the strength with which I held the handle.

After facing some trouble, I opened the door, went outside and closed it behind me. Then, I locked it with the key. When I moved, I recalled that I had forgotten the key at the door handle.

So I got back again, took it and put it in my pocket. I walked quietly toward the elevator then I remembered it was out of order.

After that, I went towards the stairs and descended them slowly, which was not my habit. My hand slipped on the filthy trail, which was not cleaned for centuries probably. I felt something hurting my hand. When I looked, I saw that my hand was bleeding because of the remaining shattered glass on the trail. I cursed my carelessness and looked at my hand with anger mixed with disappointment, combined with astonishment and tainted by anguish.

I ascended the stairs again, feeling a sensation of rupture within me. I began cleaning my wound while my internal groans were intensifying; I felt bitterness in my throat, although I did not know its source. I finished cleaning the wound, but it still pained me. I came to the conclusion that there were still some pieces of shattered glasses inside my hand. I had to go to the doctor so that no complications would occur. I changed my clothes and looked at the clock to find that it was eight twenty. I sat on the sofa in front of the apartment door, waiting for Mohab. I closed my eyes and felt like my soul was escaping my body.

I woke up, thinking I did not sleep much.

I looked at the clock; it was past three. I was surprised that I didn't have Mohab's phone number. Actually, I shouldn't be taken aback since I only knew little about him.

There is nothing worse than waiting; minutes and seconds pass by slowly and tediously, making you feel depressed. I cursed Mohab and his warnings about not going out. I imitated the way he talked to me on the phone; "Do not go out ever; I may come at any moment". What made me wait was my strong desire to see Amir and Mofek.

Dalia called me and reassured me; she told me that she was doing her best to win the championship. She said that if she qualified to the final game, she would be in Egypt in more than a week. Moreover, she admitted that she missed me. I wished she was with me at that moment; I wanted to hug and kiss her because I missed her.

Only few minutes remained before midnight. Yet, Mohab still haven't showed up. It was obvious that he wanted me to stay at home. As expected, neither Mohab nor Amir and Mofek would come. I went too far with my imagination that I started thinking he was the one, who put the shattered glasses on the trail to harm me, but why did he want me to stay at home? What was the goal behind that? If only Khaled could help me, but he couldn't even help himself.

The clock ticked, announcing the arrival of midnight .I opened the small bag where I kept my medicines and swallowed some pills without checking their names or shapes. After few minutes, the tranquilizers started giving their effects and my eyes started getting dizzy, while my head was spinning around. After few moments, I completely lost my consciousness.

Once again, the faces were without any countenances. Dalia disappeared and so did my father, after his failure to penetrate the iron fence. The only thing that remained was the screams of my mother. I saw from afar Anya; she was taking her clothes off; I tried not to look at her naked body, but she vanished after undressing her clothes entirely.

I woke up willingly, since I had no desire to continue having that dream. In fact, I didn't want to do anything at all.

I waited for few minutes before leaving the bed, since I felt unbalanced. I considered doing anything that could help me escape my miserable situation, a situation that was the outcome of my agreement with Mohab. Yasser had a training session today, he was probably training now.

I watched Yasser as he was skillfully dribbling the players. At that moment, I silenced my shout, given that Sherief tackled Yasser violently with the aim of hurting him. The spectators rushed to check on Yasser, while Sherief stood motionlessly, saying, "I didn't mean any harm."

We waited a lot for the doctor to come. The doctor conducted a quick check up on Yasser. Then he called the ambulance to move Yasser to the hospital. He was sobbing bitterly because of the severity of the pain. His parents came and the sad picture was completed.

I could not forget the look Yasser's mother gave me; it was as if I were responsible for everything that happened to her son. I withdrew from the room quietly. I asked the doctor about Yasser's medical condition and he said that Yasser would never play soccer again. I left without uttering any comment, since I was shaken by the news.

Numerous calamities have fallen upon me consecutively, as if my end was nearing.

11

No words could possibly describe my situation. I have suffered consecutively from seatbacks; it was as if God was punishing me for missing my appointment with Adel.

I feel like the worst is yet to come.

I spent three days at home. I did not want to go out, because my condition was worsening; I heard overlapping voices. I heard Adel's voice while he was talking to me about different topics, and I also heard the voice of Khaled. The only person with whom I had a long conversation was Mohab, who was smiling, conceivably happy because of my situation. When I tried to reach him, he vanished and reappeared in another room. He was determined to drive me mad.

"You are no longer the honest friend, who occupied my imagination. Curiosity was one of the reasons that helped me win the bet"

"Bet…... what bet?"

"You see, although your condition does not allow you to speak, your curiosity gets the best of you. Anyways, I will tell you everything since the match has ended"

"I know very well that you love Adel, and I also know that you promised yourself to never stop visiting him. My challenge began here; I decided to prevent you once from visiting Adel and I succeeded easily."

"Nonsense! My visit is not the only proof of my remembrance of Adel"

"That was what you thought. I know all your thoughts and I know that it was the only thing that reminded you of Adel, after you owned his beloved Dalia. Do not deny it? I told you before I know what you are thinking of. By the way, I gave you enough time to recover your health and become a stable person. In the past, I targeted your weaknesses and used them to my advantages. But now, since my rivals have no chance of winning, I only penetrate the lives of stable people and start bets with them. Through these bets, I change the course of their lives, you know, I sometimes correct their mistakes and in other times, I make the right things in their lives go wrong. You will certainly not see me again. The last thing I would like to tell you is that I'm sad because I wasted my time with you"

Throughout the period of the conversation, I looked at the ceiling of the room as if I was not interested in what he was saying. What truly saddened was that I ruined Yasser's dream, but how could I know that all this would happen?

The greatest disaster was Dalia's absence; I was the one who encouraged her to travel, since she was afraid of planes. Although she didn't qualify to the final match, she was extremely happy that she reached that advanced level. She told me she was going to come, but she was going to be a little late, because her flight was delayed. "Do not worry if I'm late for some time" she was too late; she still hasn't arrived yet.

Am I the reason why the dreams of Yasser collapsed? Am I responsible for Adel's death too? I was putting unbearable blame on myself; I was being too harsh on myself.

My parents called; they said that they had brought everything I needed, my mother told me, "I found what you want". They informed me that they were coming in two days and they did not want to see me in such state. I thought for few moments, then I wore my clothes and decided to visit Yasser.

I should be by his side now, so that he would help me assist myself. I considered the fact that his mother didn't like me. I called him on the house phone. Fortunately, Yasser answered me; I told him that I wanted to see him. He asked me to meet him after an hour at the club and I was incredibly happy.

We sat next to the playground where he used to train. He was looking at it with disenchantment. We had a conversation about Sherief's intention. I assured him that he was intending to hurt him. I recounted to him my old story with Walid. He gazed at me for a long time, and then he told me about his desire to learn how to drive. I thought of changing the topic, but he repeated the same request again and I consented.

We went out together to the car; he sat on the front seat. I started teaching him about the brakes, oil and clutch. In less than an hour, Yasser acquired all the things I wanted him to learn. He expressed his desire to drive the car, but I told him the streets around the club were so crowded now. He kept repeating his request. Eventually, I accepted it sorely. I felt safe because Yasser was able to control the car; he drove the car for a small amount of time then I took him home and went back to my place after we agreed to meet the following day.

Yasser was exceedingly outraged, while he was watching soccer training. I felt anger was boiling up inside him. When only quarter an hour was left until the end of the training session, Yasser asked to drive the car for a small trip. We sat on the car, which was parked beside the wall of the club. Yasser pointed at car that was parked at the other side and said: "This is Sherief's father car. He waits for home there until he finishes his soccer training sessions". Yasser looked at his watch and said; "now"! He looked quickly at the door of the club, spotted Sherief coming out, and drove the car; he pressed the accelerator strongly, I just closed my eyes so that I wouldn't see the scenery.

All the people, who witnessed the accident, assured me that no one was with me in the car. I wondered why they tried to acquit Yasser. In the police station, I told the policeman everything about the story. Eyewitnesses were certain that I was mad because after hitting Sherief, I said with a glorious tone;" I killed Walid, I killed Walid" I did not feel anything after that since I fainted.

Borrowing the nurse's phone cost me a fortune; I called Kareem and asked him to come immediately to the hospital. He came on time; he was amazed by the soldier who was guarding me and refused to let him into the room. I asked the nurse to tell him to bring me my medicines from the house, she accepted after she charged me more money; she was greedy. If only circumstances were better, but what circumstances was I talking about; a calamity had just occurred and there was one way to get away with it, the way which circumstances slowly led me to and which I have waited for so long!

Kareem brought a small bag which he gave to the nurse. She emptied its content on my hand. It contained a mix of tranquilizers and Anya's medicine, which had expired. I put all the drugs in my mouth and gulped some water.

The events passed before my eyes resembling a dark, gloomy and lightless screen. It was like a frightening movie made by a perplexed director. Its only viewer slept soundly. He woke up with an agonizing anguish in his head. His head was split open, and from the hole came out Mohab. He sat on the edge of my bed and mocked me.

I closed my eyes to hear his voice, "I know you are still curious even when you are nearing your end. I will tell you something so that my voice would be the last thing you heard. Do you want to know what happened to Amir and Mofek?! One of them died and the other committed suicide."

The circle narrowed down gradually. The pieces of Mohab's countenances assembled and then the features disappeared again. At this moment, I could run and escape the circle because bodies vanished and only heads remained.

Dogs' heads were cut off; their necks were throbbing lively and greasy dark blood poured from them. The dogs' heads chased after me without their bodies. I ran lengthily until fatigue got the best of me and stopped. When they approached, I ran again. I tumbled; the dogs' heads came closer to me, opened their jaws to devour me, I closed my eyes because I didn't want to witness my end.

Dark tears dropped from my eyes; the dim tears were boiled on my face. The headless dogs formed their shapes in the heated tears; they looked for their heads in the burning flames of decomposition, where the shattered parts of my body rested on the lap of my lame mother. I swum in the tears of my mother, away from Mohab, Khaled, Adel, Mofek, Sherief, Walid, and Amir, I swum away from all that cursed noise.

"The End"

Cairo , October 10th, 2010

About the author:

Aly Kotb, born in Gharbia Governorate, is an Egyptian novelist and engineer. He's earned Master's degree in irrigation from Helwan University in 2021. Aly has published four novels: "All I know", "A Parallel Woman", "Meccano" and "Waiting". Some of his stories were also published in short stories collections like; "Mystery in Old Egypt" and "He always remembers her". Some of Aly's work was directed to children, as he wrote short stories for kids in "Aladdin" and "Qatr Al-Nada" magazines. Furthermore, he translated "The Tale of Peter Rabbit" from English to Arabic. In addition to his literary works, Kotb writes articles in several websites like; Qafilah, Manshoor, El7ekaya, Alketaba.

Through the past ten years, Aly's literary work has received some notable awards such as: Ministry of Youth and Sports Award, Sawiris Cultural Award, Ihsan Abdel Quddous Award, IRead Organization's Award for historical story, Supreme Council of Culture Award for literary talent, Aden Studies Center and German GIZ Foundation Honoring Award, Egyptian Universities Award for best short story, Helwan

University Award for best short story (for 4 years in a row), Arab Culture Salon Award for best novel and Youth Centers Award for best short movie.

Aly Kotb has studied dialogue and script writing under the supervision of Dr. Medhat El-Adl and Mohamed Hefzy. Aly has participated in writing and producing "Kind Spirit" short movie, which received more than 15 awards from international film festivals.